# SMOKING GUNS

# MAX BRAND®

# SMOKING GUNS

## A James Geraldi Duo

**THORNDIKE**
CHIVERS

This Large Print edition is published by Thorndike Press®, Waterville, Maine USA and by BBC Audiobooks, Ltd, Bath, England.

Published in 2004 in the U.S. by arrangement with Golden West Literary Agency.

Published in 2004 in the U.K. by arrangement with Golden West Literary Agency.

U.S. Hardcover 0-7862-6461-6 (Western)
U.K. Hardcover 0-7540-6952-4 (Chivers Large Print)
U.K. Softcover 0-7540-6953-2 (Camden Large Print)

The text of this Large Print edition is unabridged.
Other aspects of the book may vary from the original edition.

Set in 16 pt. Plantin by Al Chase.

Printed in the United States on permanent paper.

**British Library Cataloguing-in-Publication Data available**

**Library of Congress Cataloging-in-Publication Data**

Brand, Max, 1892–1944.
   [Geraldi in the haunted hills]
   Smoking guns : a James Geraldi duo / Max Brand.
     p. cm.
   Contents: Geraldi in the haunted hills — Smoking guns.
   ISBN 0-7862-6461-6 (lg. print : hc : alk. paper)
   1. Geraldi, James (Fictitious character) — Fiction.
2. Outlaws — Fiction. 3. Large type books. 4. Western
stories. I. Title.
PS3511.A87S549 2004
  813'.52—dc22
                                       2004044030

# TABLE OF CONTENTS

# Editor's Note

Frederick Faust wrote a total of ten stories about James Geraldi, all of which appeared in various issues of Street & Smith's *Western Story Magazine* under the byline Max Brand. Two of the Geraldi stories were published as serials in a number of installments. "Three on the Trail" appeared as a six-part serial in *Western Story Magazine* (5/1/28 – 6/16/28) and was the first of the two serials to appear in book form as *The Killers* (Macaulay, 1931) by George Owen Baxter. "The Geraldi Trail" appeared as a four-part serial in *Western Story Magazine* (6/11/32 – 7/2/32), but its first book appearance was complicated by the fact that Dodd, Mead & Company, which was publishing Faust books at the time under the byline Max Brand, did not want to publish a Max Brand novel featuring a character that had already appeared previously in a George Owen Baxter novel issued by a competitor. Therefore, the character's name was changed from James Geraldi to Jesse Jackson, and the book published by Dodd, Mead in 1932 was accordingly titled *The Jackson Trail*.

*Gunman's Goal* (Five Star Westerns, 2000) — as the serial, "Three on the Trail" has now been titled — is the first story in the saga about James Geraldi, *The Geraldi Trail* (Five Star Westerns, 1999) the second. *The Bright Face of Danger* (Five Star Westerns, 2000) contains the first three interconnected stories in Geraldi's pursuit of several priceless Egyptian jewels. *The House of Gold* continues Geraldi's adventures in the next three stories. With the publication of the two final entries contained here — "Geraldi in the Haunted Hills" and "Smoking Guns" — the James Geraldi saga, at last, has been published for the first time in book form in definitive texts so they can be read as parts of a continuing saga — which was ultimately the author's intention in writing them.

# Geraldi
# in the Haunted Hills

# I

## "TWO FINGERS"

Everything that could warm the heart of a cowpuncher appeared on display along the walls or under the glass-topped cases of Mr. Michaels, the pawnbroker. There were bridles of parti-colored horsehair work, silver *conchos,* spurs, saddles curiously carved and ornamented; revolvers, plain, pearl-handled, some few set with small jewels; lofty sombreros banded with gold or silver Mexican work; boots with gorgeous tops; a whole case of hunting knives; stickpins, cuff links, rings; quirts of intricate form and decoration. He could find here presents for his lady love, as well — for there were *mantillas,* sashes, Spanish combs, watches, dainty heels for dancing slippers — everything, in fact, that could tempt the eye of a pretty range girl, or a robber.

Over this treasure, Mr. Michaels ruled with a strong hand and watched with a cold, quick eye. He knew that every man in the town envied him his wealth and hated him

11

for all his personal qualities, but envy and hatred merely sharpened the tooth of hunger-stricken Michaels. The deep disgust with which others viewed him troubled him not at all, but being in a hateful business, he was almost at pains to complete the picture by making himself hateful as well.

At this moment he was mildly disturbed, because he was about to make a small purchase to add to his stock, while a prospective customer at the same time lounged along his walls or idled by his cases. The purchase was very small that Michaels now bargained for; the customer, on the other hand, looked as though he would buy much, and at a price to suit the salesman. He was a dapper young man, darkly handsome, dressed with foolish richness in the Mexican style. The very sash that girdled his hips would be worth the price of twenty cows; the tobacco of which he made his cigarette burned with an odd sweetness. From these small signs Mr. Michaels drew his assumption of excellent business. Above all, the youth had been drinking too much. He smiled vacuously; his eyes wandered; his step was distinctly uncertain.

The second client in the shop was a desert-dried cowpuncher offering for sale a pair of golden spurs. They were of the type that cowboys love — with long spoon handles, and big rowels, and little jingling, woven chains that help to make a man's step musical when he is out of the saddle.

"Four dollars," said Michaels.

"I paid more'n a hundred," said the other.

"Five dollars," said Michaels.

"I gotta have more'n that. I count on ten dollars, anyway. Five ain't no good to me. . . ."

"You'll take five, or nothing," said Michaels.

His grim eye wandered toward the gilded youth, who had picked up a walking stick with an ivory head, traced with gold. It had cost Michaels three dollars, was worth forty, and he conservatively priced it at seventy-five for the benefit of the stranger. That would give him a margin for bargaining.

Then he spoke again to the man of the desert.

"You'll take five or nothing," he said.

"It's worth. . . ."

"It's worth five dollars. I'm a busy man," said Michaels. "Take the money or leave it. I don't care!"

This careless indolence made the other flush a deep red. Slowly his lips parted, as though the hinges of his jaws were rusted fast. Then he checked the first words as they swelled in his throat. Like many another man, he remembered that he had come here expecting money, not courtesy.

"Well . . . ," he said, and pushed the spurs forward.

He of the gaudy Mexican attire had swayed closer during the last part of this interview, and now he spoke unexpectedly.

"They're worth a hundred," he stated. "I'll lend you twenty on 'em."

He put a broad-faced double eagle into the hand of the desert rider, and the fingers of the latter closed over the money with a hungry eagerness.

"Thanks!" the cowpuncher said. "This here cold-blooded Gila monster . . . thanks!"

He extended the spurs with a faint grin, but the other shook his head.

"It's a loan, partner," he explained, "and I don't want security."

"I'm ridin' out of town," protested the cowpuncher, "and if we don't meet up. . . ."

"Those spurs wouldn't jingle right for twenty dollars," said the other. "You take 'em along, and maybe our trails will cross again."

He waved his hand, signifying that the interview had lost interest for him, and went with the same unsteady step toward the glass cases once more.

Mr. Michaels followed him like a hawk intent on prey. The cowpuncher, after hesitating for a moment, with a look that said that the business was not satisfactorily ended from his point of view, turned abruptly and left the shop, only lingering for an instant when his hand had fallen upon the knob of the door. Then, with a shrug of his shoulders, he went out to the street.

His benefactor, in the meantime, picked a knife that once must have belonged to a border dandy of the first water, for a big uncut emerald was stuck into the butt of the knife.

Mr. Michaels raised a hand to his face and coughed to cover a smile. Two hundred, tentatively, would make an asking price.

"A beautiful knife in the hand," said the stranger. "But how is it in the air?"

"In the air?" asked Michaels, frowning.

"Like this," said the other, and tossed the knife high above his head.

It whirled faster than the eye could follow. If, in falling, the jewel was broken! Mr. Michaels set his teeth, and his nostrils expanded. He hated all fools, but drunken fools particularly.

Down came the knife like a shot toward

the top of the glass case, and Michaels stepped back to avoid flying splinters. Yet the knife did not strike, for the slender hand of the stranger darted out, picked the handle from the flashing circle of steel, and shot the knife up again.

"Heavy in the grip," he commented, taking the weapon out of the air again as securely as though he were lifting it from velvet, and he replaced it in its row.

Michaels remained well back from the case, at watch. The drunkenness had been a sham, he could see. A man more sober than this never before had been in his shop, and Michaels was prepared for trouble. He himself believed that a man with two faces is twice a man.

The stranger thumbed the point of another knife.

"Very sharp," he said, "but not sharp enough, perhaps, to cut a price, Michaels?"

The latter had endured enough.

"If you wanna buy," he announced, "there's my stock. If you don't wanna buy, I'm a busy man." He pointed bluntly toward the street.

"Suppose I wish to sell, however?" said the other, with a flashing smile.

Michaels narrowed his eyes. "I'm ready for any kind of business," he declared, "so long as it's quick business. If you got something in your pocket, lemme put a price on it."

The stranger nodded, and, taking out a piece of cloth, he unwrapped it. Upon the counter he exposed to the famine-lighted eye of Michaels a dozen pearls of exquisite quality and of large size. On the accurate tip of his forefinger Michaels weighed one of them.

"They look pretty good," he said. "A hundred for this one, maybe. Take the whole dozen of them at a round figure . . . say a thousand for the lot. They been in your family long?"

"An aunt of mine had them in a necklace," said the youth. "A thousand for the dozen?"

"Yes."

"It's an odd thing," said the younger man, "but she once told me that every one of these was worth more than a thousand."

"Every one?" shouted Michaels, almost honestly excited, although he knew he had heard the truth about their value. "I never heard anything as crazy as that! If you want a thousand apiece for 'em, go try to find a sale . . . it ain't in here."

"Well, then," replied the other with unshaken good nature, which seemed to be an

17

unfailing treasure in his possession, "if you don't want to pay for pearls, what about diamonds?"

He picked half a dozen from a waistcoat pocket and rattled them onto the counter.

They were large, of finest water, but rather old-fashioned in cut. Michaels bowed his head a little to study them. For an instant he looked like one subdued to prayer, and, indeed, there was nothing that brought him closer to celestial thoughts than the sight of precious stones.

At last he looked up with a sigh. He gathered together the stones — and deliberately dropped them into his coat pocket. His left hand jerked up a gun from the shelf below the cases.

"Are you going to keep them?" asked the youth.

"I'll have the sheriff come along over and have a look at 'em," replied Michaels. "And maybe they'll be some other aunt of yours that was collectin' diamonds?"

He sneered and laughed at the same moment. Avarice overwhelmed him as with a fever. He shook, and his face reddened.

"Would you call in the sheriff?" asked the youth mildly. "Would you accuse me of having stolen the pearls and the diamonds, Michaels?"

"I know you fast-fingered sneak thieves," said Michaels. "I know you by the first flash. I've got you sized up, my boy, and you'll get nothin' out of me but a bad time. Y'understand?"

He leaned a little over the case and leered at the other, savage with triumph.

The latter trailed two fingers thoughtfully across his forehead, saying: "I seem to be out of luck." He turned the fingers and moved them back in the opposite direction. "But maybe you'll change your mind?" he suggested.

Michaels, still holding the gun, watched the active fingers as though he were reading print. He began to pant, and twitched his tongue across his dry lips.

"Who are you?" he asked, his voice half a groan.

"A friend," said the other, holding out his hand.

Michaels, hesitant, accepted it, and at the first touch he started away.

"You're too young," he said. "They never would let in a kid of your age. Besides, I know most of 'em by sight. You've stolen a sign or two . . . but what's your name?"

"Geraldi," said the visitor.

# II

## " 'HERE YOU ARE AT LAST!' "

The effect of this name was to make Michaels wince as though he had been stabbed.

"Geraldi, my foot!" he blurted, but, looking closer at the other, he rubbed his eyes suddenly and added: "Geraldi it is! I . . . I. . . ."

He faltered miserably, and, thinking of the patent fraud that he had attempted to practice, his glance went down to the gun that he still kept leveled across the top of the glass case.

This he snatched away guiltily and replaced upon the shelf beneath, muttering something about a dangerous business and the necessity for keeping weapons at hand. Geraldi, however, went briskly on with his mission. He brought out several more packets of jewels and opened them under the eyes of the pawnbroker, asking a quick estimate on the value of each.

Mr. Michaels was in agony, but for once in his life he felt that it was wise to be honest, therefore he valued the gems as accurately as though he were about to sell them himself to an expert.

"This lot," he said finally, "is worth a hundred and fifteen or a hundred and twenty-five thousand, according to how you hit the market with 'em." He looked up with a sigh of envy. "It's the Naylor stuff, ain't it, Jimmy?" he inquired.

"What d'you know about the Naylor stuff?" asked Geraldi.

"What everybody in the know has heard."

"Well, then, what has everybody heard?"

"That you got into the Naylor Ranch, cracked the safe under their eyes, and came away with the stuff, and they've been trying to crock you ever since. I know something about the Naylors," he added with a sudden glow of admiration, "and I dunno how you've got this far with so much loot."

"How long will it take you to get me the cash for this lot?" Geraldi asked coolly. "A hundred thousand will do for me. You use the rest for luck."

Mr. Michaels closed his eyes and smiled like a starved man who is swallowing food. He could have the money by the next morning, or the next afternoon at the latest, but such a sum could not be raised on the spur of the moment.

With this Geraldi agreed.

"What sort of a safe have you?" he asked sharply.

"A fine thing," said Michaels. "It ain't too big to be hid, but it's too heavy to carry away. No can opener will ever crack it, and it would take a ton of soup to bust it."

Geraldi considered for a moment.

"I'll take your note for the hundred thousand," he said at last. "Just jot down . . . for value received, I owe a hundred thousand, *etcetera*. That'll have to do me, Michaels."

Perhaps some nefarious hope that had sprung into the mind of Michaels was carried away by this last suggestion, for a shadow of loss crossed his face, yet he obediently wrote down the note as it was dictated to him.

After that, moistening his lips, his eyes upon the window, he waited humbly for further orders. Geraldi contented himself with running his eyes briefly over the writing, which he put away in a meager wallet.

He nodded and started for the door, but Michaels went eagerly after him, and even touched his arm to stop him. Geraldi turned back with a slight gesture of impatience.

Michaels came close to him, with a mixture of fear and of fawning on his face.

22

"The brotherhood," he whispered, "is a long way off, Geraldi. You take a poor fellow like me, he never knows how he stands or whether he's pleasing. Maybe you could tip me off?"

Geraldi surveyed him deliberately, and flicked the ash from his cigarette before he answered: "You know the three rules, Michaels?"

"Obedience, silence, and service!"

The words came glibly on his tongue.

"Well?" said Geraldi, who knew nothing about the repute of this fellow, but wished to judge what he could by the man's own testimony.

"They never asked a thing I didn't do, and do quick," Michaels declared with fervor. "And a good word from you to one of the heads, Geraldi, would make. . . ."

"There's the third rule . . . there's the silence," Geraldi responded coldly.

Michaels winced back with one hand thrown up to his face. Never was guilt more patent than in his twisted mouth and glaring eyes.

"I ain't been talking!" he managed to falter. "If they told you. . . ."

Geraldi raised one finger, and Michaels was silent, fairly trembling in terror and in despair.

"Listen to me," said Geraldi. "Whatever you've done, they are willing to give you a second chance. You have the chance now, and it will be locked up in your own safe."

Michaels groaned with relief.

"May I never have luck," he said, "if I don't give you the best of the deal. It ain't a commission that I'm lookin' for from you, Geraldi. But a word out of you to the heads. . . ."

Geraldi waved his hand. "I'll send them a letter after I've seen you tomorrow. Good afternoon, Michaels."

He went out into the street and stood there for a moment with the sun beating strongly upon him. He was glad to have his back turned upon the shop, so that his faint smile of satisfaction should be hidden from the man inside, but he had deep reason for this satisfaction. Whatever else Michaels did in his life, it seemed reasonably certain that he would be true to this trust, even if he had to venture his own skin in defense of the jewels that had been entrusted to him.

Then Geraldi turned away and started on a tortuous course through the town. He crossed the river to the Mexican quarter, rambled under the cottonwoods, then turned back across the upper bridge to the American side of the rambling old place.

He hardly had entered the main street before the man from the desert came up beside him. He simply slowed his step a little in passing to say: "Two follerin' you. Negro and greaser."

Geraldi replied: "Who are you, partner?"

"Sam Grey," said the other, without turning his head, and went on with a swinging step.

For he had an athlete's step, long and light, and Geraldi watched him with a good deal of satisfaction; it was plain that the money given to this stranger had not been wasted; already there was a considerable return on the investment, and Geraldi, scratching a match to light a cigarette, half turned about, as though sheltering the flame more securely from the wind.

From the corner of his eye he saw them — a big Negro now sauntering very slowly up the boardwalk, with a faded blue flannel shirt open at the throat, and his hands thrust deep into his trouser pockets. There was a Mexican — to judge by the darkness of his skin and the shape of his sombrero — lingering in front of a shoe shop, admiring the second-hand shoes and boots exposed there for sale.

Geraldi walked on, but, when he had gone another block, he felt sure that the pair was no longer trailing him, even if they had been before. Either Sam Grey had been wrong in the first place, or else they had guessed at the warning that he had passed on to their quarry.

Yet Geraldi's mind was not a whit relieved. For if he was being trailed, it meant that the news of his presence in this town had been picked up and was now being conveyed to the Naylors, particularly to that lean, bent-backed spirit of evil, Pike Naylor.

In that case, how long would it be before they suspected the transfer of the jewels to Michaels? And could Michaels hold the prize against such strong hands? He shrugged his shoulders, being determined that he would not allow himself to be upset by any small matters. If the Naylors were still after him, it was more than a matter of life itself.

As this thought came to him, he pressed his left elbow gently against his side, so becoming aware of the outline of the big Colt that was hung beneath that armpit. This comforted him, and he went on with a lighter, quicker step.

He had thought that the game was ended, the Naylors hopelessly beaten and distanced, and that all he needed to do was to cash in on his wealth and enjoy life, with only a weather eye out for possible trouble in the future from his old enemies. Now the few words of Sam Grey convinced him that he was wrong.

*Who was Sam Grey?*

*What had reduced him to such desperate straits for money?*

*How had he been able to tell that the two were trailing Geraldi?*

He turned these questions in his mind, and a sense of mystery deepened in him.

It was not unpleasant. He would hardly have found a keen sense in life if there had not been constant stresses such as this.

He was crossing the street toward a shooting gallery on the farther side when a bullet whistled sharply past his ear.

He had no glimpse of the marksman, but only of a shadow withdrawing rapidly beyond the farther corner of the building. The report of the weapon caused no excitement, because of the chattering of several guns, at this moment, inside the long shed. There could not have been a better-arranged plot, if only the aim of the marksman had been a little truer. Geraldi would have fallen, and the murderer would have escaped totally unnoticed.

However, Geraldi was of no mind to let the fellow go. The kiss of the bullet in the thin air startled him back a half step. Then he bounded ahead like a deer and turned the corner of the target gallery, to find nothing before him except a vacant lot filled with shaggy brush dust-loaded from the clouds that had risen from the street and settled here.

Still he ran on, looking vengefully from side to side, but stopped as abruptly as he had begun. This was a fruitless chase that could hardly bring him anything other than a deeper and more dangerous ambush. So he turned back to the street and went straight to the hotel.

There was no doubt about the danger that he lived under the shadow of in this town. And the best way to meet it was to leave the place at once.

In that mind he passed through the front door of the hotel, but, in crossing the lobby, he heard a woman's voice saying quietly and gravely: "Here you are at last, Jimmy."

He turned, and saw the one whom of all people he least wished to meet at this moment.

# III

## "AUNT EMILY INGALL"

She was a tall, angular woman with a masculine way of setting her jaw and looking people in the eye. Geraldi went to her at once and took her hand.

"Aunt Emily," he asked, "what brought you here?"

"A train," she replied.

"I thought you were in the East."

"I should be."

After each remark her jaws closed as firmly as before, and her eyes bored at Geraldi.

"If you don't like to answer questions," Geraldi said good-naturedly, "I'll answer while you ask."

"Are you an American, James Geraldi?" she demanded.

"I hope so."

"Then why are you dressed up like a silly Mexican dandy? You've even stained your skin . . . with black-walnut juice, I suspect."

"I like flashy things," said Geraldi.

29

"And a darker skin?"

"It protects one from sunburn, Aunt Emily."

Perhaps a glimmer of a smile came into her eyes.

"I know I'll never get anything out of you in words," she admitted. "Why do I try? But I'll keep on for a moment."

"Do," said Geraldi. "Suppose we sit down?"

"Very well. Here's a chair."

"There are a couple of better ones in that corner, where we can be more private."

He led her to the place he suggested, and she sat down, remaining stiffly erect, with her gloved hands folded in her lap. There was a moment of silence between them — an enforced silence because of an outbreak of shouting and laughter and loud whoops that swept down the street outside the little hotel as a band of cowpunchers came in off the range to stir up trouble and amusement.

Aunt Emily employed this time industriously in the scanning of Geraldi's face, and he endured the survey as well as he could.

Then she said: "Suppose I begin at the beginning."

"Thanks," said Geraldi, "and then I'll know how far you've come."

The flicker of amusement appeared again

in her eyes, but was lost in shadow once more.

"I want to know if you're engaged to marry my niece, Mary Ingall?"

"I am," Geraldi said with equal gravity.

"Do engaged young men suddenly disappear in thin air?"

"Sometimes they go to hunt their fortunes," he replied.

"And say nothing about their travels?"

"You mean, write letters?"

"Exactly that."

"Suppose a man is far away from mail boxes?"

"For a month?"

"For a month," he assented.

"Have you been away on a cruise? Have you been fenced up on a desert island, James Geraldi?"

He pointed out the window at the brown mountains that leaned back into the hazy, pale sky. They glimmered with the heat of the sun as it smote on the bald rocks, pricked only here and there with a scanty vegetation. And he smiled as he studied them.

"There are desert islands out there, Aunt Emily," he said, "where a fellow could be marooned for a year as easily as a month."

"Islands surrounded by sand?" she asked

31

him in her sharp, aggressive way.

"That and other things."

"Things as thin as danger, Jimmy, perhaps?"

"Some of that, too."

"And you've been swimming about in it for a whole month?" She snapped her bony fingers. "We're talking very high in the air, Jimmy," she added. "Suppose we come down to earth and you tell me what on earth has kept you these four weeks, while Mary has been growing pale?"

"Is Mary much troubled?"

"The second week you were ill . . . the third week you were dying . . . and the last ten days you've been lying dead on your back somewhere with the buzzards standing on your forehead. Mary has an imagination, Jimmy, and you've given it plenty of time to work."

"The fact is," said Geraldi, "that I didn't have enough money to support her."

"She didn't think she was marrying a millionaire. She expected you to work, I suppose. She's willing herself to work, for that matter, you know."

Geraldi interlaced his lean fingers, and his smile flashed at her in a way she could well remember from the old days when this strange young man was wooing and winning

Mary Ingall. Indeed, the mere sight of that smile made the old scenes, the old dangers, flood back upon her memory. It had been like a reincarnation of a tale from the *Arabian Nights*, a thing not to be believed when once it was around the corner from the eye. But now he sat before her again, and plunged her at once into the atmosphere of excitement. Anything was possible so long as this youth was near.

"I've thought over all sorts of work," he told her. "What could I do? I'm not a lawyer, a doctor, or a journalist. I'm not a farmer, a cattleman, or a miner. I'm not a sailor, a financial gambler, or a real-estate speculator. What could I do to make a living?"

"Take a job," she said. "Better men have done that."

Geraldi stirred a little in his chair.

"You're not happy at the idea," she suggested.

"I'm a lazy man, Aunt Emily," he confessed.

"Well, what did you do?"

"I went out prospecting," he told her slowly, as though he wished purposely to allow her to see that he was not telling her the entire truth. "And I struck it rich."

She repeated after him: "You went out

prospecting . . . and you found what? Gold?"

"Or things that can be turned into gold," he assured her.

She waited, examining him as though he were a strange creature first seen at this moment.

"You might have played dice, or poker, or held up a banker, or cracked his safe, or robbed a train . . . how can I tell what you've done, Jimmy?"

"Only you're sure that it wasn't honest?"

"Not sure. But the easy, quick ways usually aren't the honest ones!"

Geraldi paused, looking toward the ceiling. Certainly the Naylors, who had amassed the fortune that he had taken from them by cruelty, extortion, robbery, murder itself, had no more human right to it than he.

Then he said: "I'll tell you . . . nobody in the world has a better right than I have to the money I've collected."

"Is it enough to live on?"

"Enough to start a living."

"But not enough to keep you safe?"

"What do you mean?"

"I mean that you have to sit in a corner, at this moment, because you're afraid to have a door or a window at your back."

He made his expression perfectly innocent, then suddenly laughed at her.

"You see through everything," he said.

"You are in danger now?"

"Everyone's in danger every minute, for that matter," he said. "A tile may fall from a roof, or a trap door give way, or a pin prick turn to blood poisoning. . . ."

"Stuff!" she interrupted. "You're in danger of guns and knives, and you very well know it. But I've something more to tell you in the way of news."

"About Mary?"

"Yes. I didn't come here alone."

"Is Mary here?" cried Geraldi, his eyes shining suddenly, his whole face growing boyish and flushed with excitement.

Emily Ingall watched him with satisfaction.

"You're fond of her," she admitted. "She's too good for you, Jimmy, but for that matter she's too good for any man. I'm glad that you love her."

"But how far away is she?" asked Geraldi. "Where . . . ?"

"She's here in this hotel."

"Here!" Geraldi exclaimed, on his feet now.

"Yes. I'll take you up to her. She'll be a happy girl to see you again."

Geraldi, however, looked far away through the window with a sudden frown and seemed to fall into an instant's gloomy brooding, from which he aroused himself with a start, muttering: "Nothing could happen to her! Not in the broad daylight."

"Nothing could happen to whom? To Mary?" asked Emily Ingall. "She can take care of herself, thank you! And in broad daylight, with a whole town in hearing distance. . . . Tush, Jimmy! However, it makes me wonder what sort of people are on your trail just now, you rascal."

He smiled rather faintly at her, and they hurried up the stairs together.

"How did you find me?" he asked her on the way.

"It was nine-tenths luck. We had sense enough to come into your own country, and we put up at El Paso. That was to be the center from which we'd look around."

"And you spotted me from there?" he asked with a real wonder.

"Why, yes. You haven't been as secret as all that, you know."

"Haven't I?" he murmured with a lift of his eyebrows.

"Did you think you had? At any rate, we ran into old Mister Dakyns, your friend. We met him in the lobby of the Paso del Norte."

36

"And he told you?"

"Yes. Of course."

She heard the teeth of Geraldi click, and, as they reached the upper hall, he walked swiftly before her, so that she was panting as she hurried to catch up.

His hand was raised to knock at the door, but he stepped back without rapping; she saw that he was pale, in spite of the tint on his skin.

"You knock, Aunt Emily," he said briefly.

She obeyed. Twice she repeated the signal, but there was no answer. Then, with a wild look over her shoulder at Geraldi, she thrust the door open.

The room was empty!

# IV

## "PURCHASED BY THE NAYLORS"

All was in order, the two beds were made, the two suitcases closed. Some toilet things lay shining on the top of the bureau, brightly reflected in the mirror above it, and on the windowsill stood a glass filled with yellow wildflowers. There was even a faint perfume in the air, and almost a breathing presence in the room, but Mary Ingall was not there.

Geraldi, for one instant, stood on the threshold and surveyed these things, then he whirled and was down the stairs with a leap. Emily Ingall heard his feet crash on the landing, then in the hallway. The next moment a screen door banged.

She followed as fast as she could run, and issued into the back yard of the ramshackle old hotel, to find Geraldi in quick conversation with the stableman.

"They left down that way," he was explaining. "The old gent was sayin' that they'd better hurry along, and the girl was willin'. What's wrong?"

Geraldi did not answer, but fled into the interior of the stable. Emily Ingall followed him, and, as he flung saddle and bridle upon a gleaming black horse, he fired questions at her.

"This Dakyns . . . what was the look of him?"

"He was tall, very old, and bent in the shoulders. He looked eighty, but tough and strong as fifty, say, with white hair. . . ."

"Pike Naylor," Geraldi said through his teeth, and drew up the cinches so hard that the horse grunted.

"Who is Pike Naylor? And what's become of Mary? Jimmy, Jimmy, the man was never made that would harm Mary!" cried her aunt.

"You don't know who made the Naylors," he replied, and rushed out of the stable on the back of the horse.

She saw him dart down the alley and disappear with a swerve into the street, the dust spurting like water as the horse nearly lost footing, and then desperately regained it.

The stableman looked after him with a nod of satisfaction.

"Now there's a gent," he said, "that knows how to throw a hoss around a corner. I seen Injuns do it. I seen greasers like him do it. But I never seen a white that knowed proper how to get a hoss around a quick turn. What's eatin' him, ma'am?"

"He's trying to follow Mary Ingall," she told him, taking possession of herself with a great effort. "Did you hear the man who was with her say anything that would suggest a direction?"

"Hello!" he exclaimed. "Was the old boy crooked? He had a kind of a hard look. Why, he didn't say much, except that Jimmy would be down by the river, and they could surprise him . . . something like that, and her askin' if Jimmy was well, and lookin' pleased and mighty pretty. A lucky gent is this Jimmy, I reckon, if he ain't just a brother to her."

Emily Ingall went back to the hotel and up to the empty room. She kept her face steady and tried to clear her mind of worry, but thoughts of the girl leaped into it like knife thrusts, more swiftly than she could parry.

A long hour passed, and then up the street she saw the black horse coming, now gray with dust except where the sweat washed streaks of it away. Geraldi sat as lightly, as erectly in the saddle, as ever. But she guessed that it was not joy of heart that kept him so proudly straight.

He came up to the room to see her at once, and stood by the window, winding and unwinding the lash of his quirt. He controlled his voice perfectly, even making it gentler than usual, but she knew that fear and rage possessed him.

She hardly dared to ask what they should do, and he answered her: "We'll have to wait."

"And Dakyn's . . . Naylor, you called him? What could he dare to do with Mary?"

Geraldi explained calmly: "Naylor is the mine out of which I dug my money. He wants it back. He's taken Mary. His idea is an exchange."

"Than thank heaven for that!" she said. "Jimmy, I've been sitting here in a dreadful torment, imagining . . . but it'll be all right. You'll give back what you took from the man. . . ."

"I don't know that I shall."

"You don't know?" she gasped, her self-control suddenly gone.

"Blackmail's an ugly thing," Geraldi stated.

"Worse then theft?" Emily Ingall cried sharply.

He looked at her without resentment. He was cold as iron.

"A man risks something when he steals," said Geraldi. "The stealing of Mary, for instance, I don't resent. A good brave thing, in a way. Old Pike stood an excellent chance of having a bullet through his head. But he slipped in and got her away while you and I were . . . talking. Sitting and talking!"

He laughed a little, in a way that made the hearer shudder.

"However, blackmail is a different matter," he added.

"I want to understand you," she said. "I want to *try* to understand you. You mean that you'd let my darling Mary stay in the hands of a man. . . ."

"I mean that I'll try to find her," he said shortly.

"Jimmy, I can see that you're furious. I know that you have a right to be. But you won't let anger cloud your mind? You'll take everything into consideration?"

"I'm trying to."

"If you couldn't find the trail of the man now, how can you later on?"

"They'll have to send me a message."

"Offering terms, d'you mean?"

"Exactly. Appear at the bridge at midnight with a chamois leather bag in your hand and with no companions. Put the bag on the stump at the head of the bridge. Oh, I know exactly how the note will read. In return, I get Mary back. That's a simple thing, isn't it? But I don't like blackmail."

"I want to understand you, Jimmy," said Aunt Emily. "But don't let me think for a moment that you'd give up Mary."

"I don't want you to think it," he told her. "Of course, I wouldn't. On the other hand . . . blackmail. It's like threatening a man's child in order to make him come to time. It's the most poisonous thing that I know anything about. Mary? I don't know. I'm going to see."

He left Aunt Emily, and went straight out through the town, walking down the main street with a fixed smile on his lips and murder in his heart. He walked slowly, carelessly, with his hands continually occupied in the rolling of cigarettes — but all the while his nerves were on edge, as he waited and watched for a suspicious move on the part of someone near him. Once a flash made his hand jump for a gun — but it was only the drawing of a handkerchief. Again, someone sidestepped toward him in a crowd and nearly received a bullet through the heart for his pains. But finally it became evident that, if the Naylors had representatives still in the town, they were instructed to leave Geraldi alone.

He turned across the nearest bridge, and the first man he met was Sam Grey, who leaned on the railing and watched the bare-legged Mexican boys fishing, their lines hanging from long, slender poles that cast broken reflections into the water.

The golden spurs were restored to the boots of Sam Grey. A new sombrero rested upon his head, pushed back at a pleasantly careless angle, and an air of rest possessed him. Geraldi paused at his side.

"I haven't thanked you for giving me the word," said Geraldi.

"There ain't any call," replied Grey.

He turned and faced Geraldi with his bright, steady, gray eyes. The lids had been puckered by many an hour of contraction to shut out the glare of the desert sun. Now he took a double eagle from his pocket and extended it in the palm of his hand.

"And here's yours back ag'in," he said.

"You don't need it now?" asked Geraldi.

"I don't need it," said Sam Grey.

"I'm glad you've stepped into a paying game," Geraldi said, and took his gift back. He was surprised by this sudden change in the other's fortunes, but he kept his surprise under cover.

"Sure," said Grey, with a sneer that was obviously directed at himself rather than at Geraldi. "I struck it tolerable rich. Through you, Geraldi."

"I didn't know we were acquainted by name."

"No more, we wasn't. I picked up the information and some loose change at the same time."

Geraldi watched him in silence for a clearer explanation, and Grey gave it with astonishing frankness.

"They figgered that I might sit in on your side of the table," he explained. "And so they come and offered me a price, and I'm a hired man, ag'in. Only, I don't have to do nothin'. I'm paid for not doin' nothin'."

His bitterness at himself broke out in a subdued muttering of oaths, but he ended by shrugging his shoulders.

"Well, then, I ain't a saint, and you know the truth about it, Geraldi. Which don't stop me appreciatin' you none."

"They bought you up?" asked Geraldi. "They did a good job. If I had you, old-timer, I might have bothered them a good deal more. They knew you'd given me the tip when you passed me on the street?"

"They guessed at it. They got brains and eyes and ears everywhere, it looks like." Then he added in a slightly changed voice: "Mind you, Geraldi, I've put my cards on the table. I've told you that I'm on the other side."

"I understand. It's square of you to let me know."

"And after this I ain't talkin' so free."

Geraldi nodded again. He shook the hand of Sam Grey.

"I wish I had you with me," he said briefly. "But as long as they have you, I wish you luck."

He went back from the bridge toward the hotel again, feeling that he had walked into deeper trouble than ever. He had respected the brains and the cunning of Pike Naylor before this, but he had not suspected the spreading power and the many hands with which the old man could work.

For his own part, he felt that he had been backed against a wall, and that there was hardly a way out of the tangle. There had been enough force against him before this. But such a man as Sam Grey almost doubled the opposing strength. He recognized it with a gloomy conviction that he was entered in a lost game, and yet he would not surrender. What he could do he could not tell; at least, he could hold on, as the bulldog does, until it dies.

The heat of the day softened, and in the cool of the evening he turned up the dusty street on which the hotel stood. Two women were walking toward him, and one of them reminded him with odd force of the angular figure of Aunt Emily Ingall. She came nearer, and suddenly he was convinced that it was she. Her companion, in the meantime, hurried ahead, and Geraldi stopped short, feeling that he had gone mad.

For it was Mary Ingall that he saw before him!

# V

# "GERALDI'S HUMILIATION"

To Geraldi it was as though he were seeing her for the first time. The crowded events that had filled his mind since he was last with her now became no more than a whiff of smoke dissolving in the wind, and Mary Ingall was the only reality. With both her hands in his, his eyes dwelling on her hungrily, he wondered how he could have left her for an instant. The danger through which she had just passed made her still more charming in the eyes of Geraldi.

Aunt Emily walked slowly on; the two younger people followed.

"Old Naylor turned his back one instant, and you were off, Mary?" he asked her.

She shook her head. "He let me fly, but kept a string attached," she said.

"A string attached?" asked Geraldi, instinctively frowning as he looked back over his shoulder.

She told her story quickly, without any waste of words and exclamations. She had ridden with the old man rapidly down to the river below the town, and there a group of four riders, having a dozen spare horses with them, came out from the willows and joined them, but no Geraldi was among them. For the first time she was suspicious, and said so. At that old Naylor dropped his mask.

"He told me," said Mary Ingall, "that you had taken money and jewels away from him and divided it among confederates. He swore that he would have back his own from the others later on, but now he wanted from you only what you had taken. He'd keep me for the exchange."

"And you?" Geraldi asked, disregarding the charges against himself as though they had not been made.

She would not allow that calm dismissal, but looked steadily up at him.

"He said that you'd robbed him," she repeated. "Is that true?"

"I did," said Geraldi. "He's lived like a hawk himself, and every penny that he has is built up from robbery and murder. I cleaned out his safe for him. Was that wrong?"

"You know it was wrong, Jimmy," she told him. "What right had you to take the law into your own hands?"

"Gamblers," he replied cheerfully, "ought to expect that other people may try to get into the game. If people mark cards, marked cards are apt to be run in on them. That's plain and simple justice, I should say."

She shook her head, but still she could not help smiling.

"I want to know what happened when Naylor and his bandits were around you," he continued.

"He pointed out that it would be easy for him to take me wherever he pleased, and he knew that you would pay what you could to have me back again. But he said it would blacken him a great deal to have it known that he was a kidnapper, and it would put me into a great deal of anxiety to be taken away by strange men. . . ." She paused and grew a trifle pale. "They looked like the worst ruffians in the world!" she added.

"And so," Geraldi conjectured, "he asked you to come back and use your influence with me to restore the money? That doesn't sound like the Pike Naylor I know. He's never trusted words before."

"He asked me to promise to come and tell you what he had said, and, if I couldn't persuade you to send him back the money, I gave him my word of honor that I'd return to him."

"Was that it?" asked Geraldi. "Did the old scoundrel trust to that?" He laughed a little as he spoke. Then he continued: "But he forgot that you might be prevented from returning to him, Mary."

"By you, Jimmy?" she asked with dangerous quiet.

"And why not?"

"I don't think you'd do that," she replied. "You're as brave a man as lives, I know, as clever a man, and all that . . . but I don't think you'd use your courage and your cleverness to make me break my word. I shook hands with him on it, Jimmy."

"If you go back," Geraldi said, after a moment of pondering, "which way are you to ride?"

"I can't tell you that. You shouldn't ask me."

"Great heavens," exclaimed Geraldi, "one might think that you're working for Pike Naylor!"

"I am," she said. "I'm trying to persuade you that I'm worth money . . . quantities of it . . . loads of cash. I'm trying to persuade you to balance me against a bank account, Jimmy!"

He acknowledged the force of the irony

with a slight gesture.

"You're hard on me, Mary," he said.

"I'm begging for my freedom," she answered. "Oh, Jimmy, don't think that I could be kept from living up to my promise. I'd starve to keep my honor bright."

"You would, I know," he murmured.

"There's no hurry," she told him. "I have till tomorrow morning to take the money to him . . . if you wish to send it with me."

"You'll have to take it?"

"Yes."

"Why not a messenger?"

"Because that would reveal the direction in which he's lying with his men, and he's afraid of you. He frankly told me that he fears you more than poison, and I don't blame him. I'm afraid of you just now. Afraid of what you'll do, Jimmy. Frankly, I am."

"And when you've brought him what he asks, how do I know that you'll be sent freely back to the town?"

"He gave me his own promise about that."

"His promise?"

"You have no right to sneer," the girl said angrily. "There are people in the world whose honor is sacred."

"From the way you speak, I don't think you include me in the list."

Her indignation softened into sorrow.

"What am I to think? You'd no sooner asked me to marry you, Jimmy, than you disappeared. To do some great thing, I thought . . . perhaps to start yourself in business of some sort, so that we could be married at once. And then I learn that you've ridden out and robbed a helpless old man."

"Helpless? D'you know that he was hedged around with twenty men, with a guard fixed to. . . ."

"What difference does it make? Robbery is robbery! Do you think I could have lived on stolen money? I'd rather breathe poisoned air!"

"I think you mean it," he replied coldly. "I'm to bring you the money, then?"

"You're to do what makes you happy, Jimmy."

"I'll send it at once. Are you taking it out now, or in the morning?"

"I'll take it at once."

"It will be here!"

He left her, and went away slowly enough to hear Aunt Emily asking: "Have you two quarreled the moment you met?"

"I've been silly," Mary Ingall answered. "But he doesn't know how I feel. I'll call him back. . . ."

"Let him go," said the older woman. "Because no man has fallen so far in love that a little discipline won't make him fall deeper."

It hardened the mind of Geraldi to hear the talk behind him, reaching his ears as it did in a total lull of the wind, in a sudden absence of all the noises of the town, as though fate had planned definitely that he should overhear this stinging portion of the conversation.

Sulkily he went on, his lips compressed, his mind tortured by a decision that he would in some way hurt the people whom he most loved. Of all emotions, self-pity is that with the sharpest edge. It wounded Geraldi unseen, and he was still cold with anger and sorrow and nameless misery when he came to the pawnshop.

He found Michaels lighting his display window, for the evening light was already too dim to show off the stock sufficiently well. Of Michaels he demanded the things that had been placed in the safe, and this brought a wail of dismay from the storekeeper. He wanted to know if he was suspected already? He swore that he would deal honestly with every item of the jewels, but Geraldi was adamant.

He did not care even to speak enough to convince poor Michaels that he was not removing the treasure owing to any suspicion of its present keeper.

So Michaels came up from his cellar presently, and gave the chamois bag into Geraldi's hands. He followed the latter to the door, fawning, almost weeping, in his anxiety, but Geraldi left with a single gruff word.

He did not cast so much as a glance behind him to see how his abrupt departure and change of plans had affected the other, but, if he had lingered near the door, he would have been amazed to see poor Michaels snatch a hat from the wall, extinguish the window lamp that he had just lighted, and, bolting and locking the front door, run out from a side entrance and so hastily, furtively, into the street.

For Geraldi was grimly bent on the thing that lay before him, and he returned to the hotel rapidly, regardless of any danger from the men of the Naylors who might be about, blinded to such a point that he almost ran under the hoofs of a horseman who was galloping down the street, and also regardless of the furious cursing that his carelessness earned from the rider.

What went on in that mind tormented with self-pity, with sulkiness, with pride, with grief, with love, with a thousand pains? He told himself bitterly that he was grievously suspected. Yet he had to admit that his actions deserved distrust. He told himself that he had risked his life a dozen times to gain the very treasure that he must now remove to Naylor. Yet the girl spoke of sheer "robbery." And she was right, he well knew. Moreover, he was treated lightly behind his back, and the women spoke together of "discipline" for him.

No prouder man ever stepped the earth than Geraldi, and now he was in a torment of rage and sullen desire to return pang for pang.

He found the two waiting for him at the hotel, with the girl's horse at the hitching rack, and her hat already on.

She greeted him with the most radiant of smiles, but Geraldi told her coldly that he had brought what they had bargained for. That was all. Except that he would ride with her, if she would change her mind. It was growing dusk — the sky showed a deep blue beyond the lighted window, with a rim of rose along the horizon. Was it right for her to go out alone?

She looked at his cold, ominous face, and shrugged her shoulders.

"I won't be frozen and frightened even by your dignity, Jimmy," she said. "I'll go alone, and I don't want to be followed. I'll be back in an hour."

# VI

## "SIX SILENT SHADOWS STRIDING"

Her horse disappeared into the warm dusk at a swinging lope, and Geraldi commenced to pace impatiently up and down.

"Why not go back to the hotel?" Aunt Emily asked.

"I'll wait here," he declared stubbornly, "for exactly one hour!"

"And then you'll leave and never come back? Is that the idea in your childish mind?"

Geraldi suddenly stopped in his pacing and threw out both hands, asking: "Why hasn't Mary your sense?"

"She would have, if she were as far from you as I am. And if I were as close to you as Mary is, I'd be more exacting, foolish, stubborn, headstrong, willful, and whimsical than she is. Do you think we can be reasonable with the people we love?"

He listened to her with a frown that gradually smoothed itself away.

"I'm going to try to hope she'll come

back," he said, "and, if she doesn't, I start on the trail after her."

"Oh, she'll come back."

"Would you bet on that?"

"You don't seriously think, Jimmy, that . . . that. . . ."

"Confound it!" exclaimed Geraldi. "Now that they've found how easy it is to blackmail me through her, d'you dream that they'll let her come back? After Pike Naylor has finished gloating for five seconds over the cash that's been replaced in his hands, he'll laugh at any idea of letting her come back here."

Aunt Emily queried: "Did you think that before she left?"

"She badgered me into letting her go."

"You're not serious about the old man?"

Geraldi groaned aloud. "He's the king of all evil! But . . . still, I'll wait here for one hour. She may have been right. There's always that chance. Pretty girls and their smiles may budge even old Pike Naylor."

He continued his walking up and down through the brush of the vacant lot at the side of which they had left Mary Ingall. Aunt Emily joined in his pacing and talked for a time, but at length grew quiet as the last of the daylight faded out, and the night came thick and powdered with its millions of small stars.

She wore a wristwatch that she consulted from time to time, covertly, yet knowing that all her movements were watched by the cat-like eye of Geraldi.

Heavily, wearily, the long hour went by them, and yet, when it came to the point when only ten minutes were left, suddenly it seemed that the seconds were flying past them with breathless speed. They saw a dozen silhouettes of riders, bobbing down the street with their heads among the stars, but none of them was Mary Ingall, and at last Geraldi paused in his walking, took off his high-crowned sombrero, and wiped his forehead with a handkerchief.

"The time's up," he announced.

"Wait ten minutes!" pleaded Aunt Emily. "Ten short minutes, Jimmy, to see if she won't. . . ."

"You don't want to be left alone with the truth," he answered. "I know that, and I'm sorry, but I've got to go out there and find her."

"What can you do in the dark, Jimmy?"

"Figure out possibilities of the direction in which they might go, and then take a chance that I'll hit on the right one with my horse."

"If you catch up, you're only one man,

and they're several, you heard Mary say. . . ." She paused. She could remember another time when more than one stood against him, and what he had done to the great odds. Yet she continued: "There's the law to call in, Jimmy."

"There's the law to be called in," Geraldi said patiently, like one explaining to a child. "And there's then a murder to be done. Keep the game privately between Pike Naylor and me, and he'll try to win . . . he'll try his blackmail system. But once let him fear for his hide, and he'll end Mary with no more compunction than he'd use in cutting the throat of a calf."

Aunt Emily gasped as she listened, and caught his arm, so that she could steady herself.

"I know you mean it, Jimmy," she said. "It's your hand against all the rest of them?"

"My hand," he said through his teeth.

But then she felt the swelling of the muscles in his arm, and a tremor of strength running over him.

"However," said Geraldi, "the dice haven't been shaken for the last time, and there's still a hope that I may be able to do something in this business. You wait here and keep your heart as high as you can. I've just hit on the right direction to ride, I think."

"What have you seen, Jimmy?"

"Something in my head. I think it can't be wrong."

"If I were a man!" Emily Ingall broke out fiercely. "Oh, if heaven would let me be man enough to ride along and help you, Jimmy!"

He laughed a little as he thanked her, and then he was gone into the darkness, moving with his quick, light stride, which was soundless on the earth, soundless even on the boards of the sidewalk.

Immediately afterward three other men moved shadow-like down the walk, and close behind them three more. Aunt Emily wondered at the similarity between them and Geraldi, and suddenly she decided that it was because their step was quick and light, like his, and silent as his was, also. Six men moving in exactly the same manner, shadow-like in their silence, amazed her. And then she realized where she had seen the same characteristics before.

They were Indians; no others moved in such a manner, except Geraldi himself. Strange that she should not have marked the similarity between them before. She wondered if there were not some strain of the Indian blood in that odd youth. His eyes and skin were dark enough, but his expression, the contours of his face, all were those of a white man.

She stepped out onto the sidewalk herself, and, staring hard through the dimness, barred as it was by the occasional shafts of light from windows and open doors, she saw Geraldi cross the street, bearing toward the hotel.

A moment later three of those same forms she had just noted crossed the street behind him. The others kept on, without crossing, but they moved more slowly.

She was puzzled for a moment. Certainly it appeared as though the six were trailing Geraldi, and whatever else she did, she could give him a warning of their coming.

She hurried straight on, walking rapidly, with a long, mannish stride that she had cultivated in tramping in the mountains many years before.

But when she was close to the hotel, she saw the black horse swing rapidly out into the street from the stables. She called out, but Geraldi went on, whether he heard or not.

Behind him all six of the Indians — if such they were — stepped into the roadway and ran off down the street.

Aunt Emily stared, and then laughed a little. She had seen mad things before in her life, but she never had heard of men running to catch up with a horse. Particularly such a horse as the black, with Geraldi on its back!

But in a moment the striding forms glimmered out of sight, and nothing was left of them to her senses except a slight taint of dust, blown down the wind.

# VII

## "SHANKS"

The anger that Mary Ingall carried with her out of the town hardly lasted until she saw the flat face of the desert before her, with the sunset dying along the distant mountains, which seemed to be drawing back from her as she galloped toward them. She was familiar with that most common of all optical illusions on the desert, but still it brought into her mind all the danger, all the dread that might be found in this land where all appeared open, but where everything was dressed with mystery as with a robe.

She checked her horse abruptly and looked over her shoulder at the town, already drawing together behind her and glimmering with friendly lights.

She never endured a stronger temptation than she felt at this moment to whirl her horse about and race it back to Geraldi. But now the thought of him, and of how she had defied him and stated her own independence, made her go doggedly ahead. It was almost as though she dared not turn back to Geraldi now, having offended him so deeply, and for the first time. It seemed to her that she had been made to act toward him as she had done, and tears of vexation rose in her eyes.

She touched her horse with her quirt, and the good animal sprang off into a full gallop. When she next glanced over her shoulder, the lights of the town had drawn into a single huddle, and out of the night before her stood up the appointed meeting place. It was merely a staggering shack, with a shed leaning against its back, a wreck of a house so very death-worn that the stars looked through its ribs.

This was the place.

She drew her horse down to a trot, and then to a walk. No one showed at the house. Not a voice sounded. There was no stamping of horses. And fear came over her more strongly than before.

At last she halted and called.

In reply a form stepped from the shapeless shadow of the doorway and advanced a few steps toward her.

"Is that you, young lady?" asked the familiar nasal snarl of Pike Naylor.

"It's I," she said. "Mister Naylor, I've brought what you want."

"And found out about my name, too, along with the rest of it? Well, well, and heard pretty many of hard things about an old man, I reckon, as well?"

He came on up to her and stood a moment, patting the neck of the mustang and nodding up at her.

"Here you are," she said, and gave the chamois bag into his hands.

"Well done, and fair and true," said Pike Naylor, clutching the sack literally to his breast as though it were a thing of flesh and blood. "No better girl than you ever stepped in these parts of the world. I'm telling you . . . and no finer, or braver, or more persuadinger, neither, if you persuaded these here right out of the pockets of Geraldi."

He laughed with a violence that made him double over and fly into a hacking fit of coughing.

"If that finishes the bargain," said the girl, "I suppose I can go home. Good night, Mister Naylor."

"Hold on! Hold on!" said Naylor. "You wouldn't be runnin' away like this before I've had the time to talk to you a minute, honey, would you, now?"

"I've got to get back," she said. "They're waiting for me."

"Her and Geraldi, eh?" asked Pike Naylor. "Jimmy Geraldi, ragin' and tearin', and gnashin' of his teeth when he thinks of what it costs a man to be in love, hey?"

He cackled again, patting the shoulder of the mustang in time with the rhythm of his laughter.

"I'll go back now," she insisted.

"No, no, honey," said Naylor. "You wouldn't be goin' back till I've had a good chance to look things over and make sure that everythin's here?"

"Let go the rein!" she commanded. But the claw of the old man was fixed fast upon it.

"Steady, steady, honey," he said. "Don't you go to excitin' of yourself and the hoss. Steady and slow is what wins the race. Everything is gonna turn out all right, if only you'll take things easy. We'll just have a mite of light on this."

He slipped his arm through the rein, and, opening the little chamois sack, he struck a light and took out the contents.

She heard him making a little crooning sound of content as he gazed at the softly glimmering beauty of the stones, and his head swayed in rhythm from side to side, adoring their wealth.

An instant later he exclaimed: "But these

ain't more'n a third of what he stole, the infernal cheat and robber!"

"You're wrong!" said the girl warmly. "Jimmy's incapable of tricks. He must have put in everything that he took . . . everything that he had of yours, at least. He would never try to cheat."

"Women and jewels. Women and jewels. There ain't a man ever been born that wouldn't cheat about 'em. Don't tell me that he wouldn't. Aye, the young fox . . . and then to send you out with 'em, expectin' me to turn you loose."

She did not wait to hear any more, but, wrenching hard against the rein, she tore it suddenly from his hold and swerved the horse away. Fast as a good cutting horse can wheel and start — and nothing of its bulk is half so nimble afoot — she drove the mustang away, with Pike Naylor's exclamation of surprise ringing in her ears. Not till she was under full way did she see that she was already in a trap.

For two horsemen sat their saddles before her, two more at either side, so as to form a wide semicircle of which the shack was the central point.

She jerked back on the reins, and the wise cow pony, understanding, squatted and skidded to a stop. The hot desert dust swept up over her, and, as it cleared, she saw that the four riders had not moved from their places.

"There, there, there," said the voice of Pike Naylor. "Skeered half to death and tryin' to get away from them that would take care of her. Come back here, honey, and you trust to your old Uncle Pike. He'll see to you."

She thought of a dozen protests; a childish desire to cry out that they would be punished for this affair had to be checked. By keeping silent, she knew that she had increased her self-respect and her dignity.

But she was more frightened than she ever had been in all her life. It was not only the danger itself that terrified her, but the memory that Geraldi had warned her against this very thing — warned her coldly and impersonally of what would happen. He was right, but would he now act to secure her from the effect of her own folly? Or would he remain gloomily in the town, waiting for her to taste the bitterness of her own mistake?

These thoughts leaped through her mind as Pike Naylor called for a horse, and one was led out to him from behind the shack by another mounted man.

A party of six horsemen was gathered about her.

She could not see them in detail; she could not be sure whether they were white or Indian, but she knew that they obeyed the will of old Pike Naylor with dangerous order, like soldiers trained to a rigorous discipline.

She was invited to ride ahead with Pike himself while the others fell in behind. For an hour the horses were kept at a strong gallop. Then a relay of fresh mounts was brought up from the rear, saddles were quickly changed, and the headlong flight began again, all in silence, except when old Pike Naylor raised his long arm as a signal for a halt and a change of horses.

The moon came up, but it was dim and useless behind a screen of clouds. All that she could see by it was Pike Naylor's silver beard jerking in the wind of the gallop. That was all.

The third hour ended with them close under the mountains, in a rolling land pricked with Spanish bayonet, with many other forms of lower-lying cactus, and with small desert shrubbery in the hollows where spring rains might run down and store a little moisture for which the long roots could drill into the sub-soil.

Presently the hoofs of the horses rang hollow and hard on a footing of naked rocks that paved the bottom of a long draw that pushed back into the upper ground. Pike Naylor halted the party again. He directed briefly that the arms of Mary should be tied behind her, at the elbow, and that the hoofs of her horse and that of his own should be bound with leather.

It was done quickly.

Quick, rough, practiced hands jerked her elbows and tied them together in the small of her back, while others muffled the hoofs of the two horses.

She heard one voice raised in question of this proceeding.

"I'm hired for work, trouble, and all that, but not for the murder of girls, Naylor."

"Who asked you to murder one, you dolt?" snarled Pike.

"Nor to give no face to no murder," said another in a louder tone.

"Sammy Grey is a good boy, and he always done what was right," said Pike Naylor, "excepting when he was south of the Río Grande. And then he sort of spread himself and had a good time. Why, don't I know enough to hang you up ten times, you desert rat, you?"

"You got a long lip," replied the disputant, "but that don't count with me. You've heard me talk, and I mean what I said. Is

71

that down with you yet, Pike?"

She turned her head eagerly, waiting for the answer. It seemed to her that she was already dying — choked by a mortal terror.

"Young feller," said Pike, "when you and me get better acquainted, you ain't gonna be fool enough to stand in between me and what I got in my mind to do. Understand that? You're gonna have a pile better sense than that. Meanwhile, back up and hold your hosses! She's gonna be safe. I ain't gonna harm her nor let harm come to her. Ain't I worried enough about Geraldi already, without givin' the young hound more cause for hating of me?"

This reassurance silenced the man called Sam Grey, but it only partly comforted the girl. She knew that Pike Naylor could lie smoothly and without pain; she was only given some ease by the reflection that there was little, apparently, to be gained by his destruction. It would accomplish no more than her release, or even less, for it might bring Geraldi more savagely upon the trail, and her freedom would tend to pacify that dauntless warrior and cunning hunter of men.

Logic, however, no matter how faultless, is a poor substitute for known facts. She could not soothe herself entirely with mere suppositions, but she vowed that she would neither yammer childish questions nor beg like a coward for mercy.

"Wait here, all of you!" Pike commanded. "I'm gonna take the girl up to Kimber Creek and leave her there with Shanks."

One of the men — perhaps it was Sam Grey — exclaimed at this, but his words were indistinguishable to Mary. She found that her horse was being led on by Pike, and for some time they wound up the rocky draw, until it narrowed and turned left into another and wilder cañon. There was a faint scent of the acrid desert brush against which the horses rubbed on either side. Big rocks and boulders rose up around them, then houses. She confused them at first with more rocks, which happened to have oddly architectural designs. Then she realized that she was riding through a silent city.

It was far more grim than passing through a great cemetery. The moon showed its face to them through the shattered rafters of what had once been a large house or barn. A hotel, perhaps. And now, as she looked more closely, she saw that some of the shacks were half fallen down, others stood straight enough, although the strong desert winds had torn away the rotting boards from the uprights.

Several times the horses trod on decayed wood that crunched softly under foot. Apparently the place had been deserted for long years — and yet she was to be entrusted to the keeping of someone in this silent wilderness of ruin.

She compressed her lips and winked the tears back from her eyes.

Now the cañon swerved to the right sharply, and, as it did so, Pike Naylor led her horse up the steep bank to higher ground. It was very hot; the air hung still and close; it touched her face like breath.

"Halloo! Shanks! Shanks, you long-legged redhead! Where are you, Shanks?"

"Damn you," said a deep, strong voice close at hand. "You goat-face, you wooden-made razor-back, you buzzard . . . I'll give you names, if you want 'em, and everybody on the range would know who I meant! I'll teach you to talk names to me, you white rat! I'll learn you something worth knowing!"

Pike Naylor did not protest against this volley of abuse. He merely replied: "I'm glad to see you, Shanks."

"You don't see me," said the voice, "and that's where you're a dolt and a liar again! But here I am now, if you wanna feast your eye on me, eh?"

She stepped out from thick bushes, and Mary saw that the owner of the gruff voice was a woman indeed. The shags of her hair fell across her face and to her shoulders. She had long legs, which apparently had given her the nickname, and arms to match them, and great, powerful, stooped shoulders, upon which her head seemed to be set without the joining help of a neck.

This female monster stepped closer to them, and placed herself straight before old Naylor.

"What's the thing with you?" she asked.

"A woman, Shanks."

"Ain't I got eyes to see that? But what kind of a woman?"

"Young, beautiful, charming, and good," Pike Naylor answered.

This tribute seemed to touch Shanks in exactly the right place, for she broke into a tremendous peal of laughter that fairly doubled her up, and Pike Naylor joined in, his high, cackling voice overriding that of the hag as the crowing of a rooster sings above the uproar of a barnyard.

# VIII

## "THE ONLY THING SHANKS FEARED"

That double burst of laughter was, strangely enough, to Mary Ingall worse than all that had gone before it — the seizure, the long ride, the mystery of the dead town, the sudden appearance of the hag herself. As a wave of hysteria sprang up to her brain, she set her teeth to keep control of herself.

An image flared in her mind, too, like an illustration out of a child's book of tales, of these two dragon-like personifications of evil, and of Geraldi, as another St. George, destroying the unclean things.

The worthy pair had no easy task finishing their burst of mirth, but continued it for some time. One would have thought that the qualities which Pike attributed to the girl were things forgotten on earth, or characteristics pretended to by hypocrites alone.

"Let's go in and have a light on everything," said Pike. "I gotta tell you a few things. You're gonna take care of this here beauty for me, Shanks."

"Lead her in," Shanks said in a more agreeable tone, now that she had laughed herself into a pleasanter humor. "Mind in front of the door, though . . . it's kind of rough goin'."

Mary Ingall, at Pike's command, slipped down from the saddle and walked beside him, his claw of a hand upon her arm, behind the long-striding woman. They turned between a couple of great rocks and came then in front of a small house into which Shanks disappeared. A match scratched and flared, then, as it was touched to the wick of a lantern that hung on the wall, almost all illumination was cut off; only the great shadow of Shanks hovered against the wall and choked the doorway in which the girl stood with Naylor. The flame rose, spread, and steadied into a constant flood of light, so that Mary could look about her.

It was the rudest of shacks. It held a stove with a rusted, staggering chimney above it, two bunks — one at either side — a broom made of mesquite fiber pounded into shreds, an axe, a broken stool, a table composed of a warped board laid over two improvised sawhorses, and very little else in the way of furniture. Some ragged clothes hung from pegs in a corner, with an old-fashioned rifle leaning close to them. This nearly completed the list of articles in the place, except for the few pots and pans on the stove.

"Look around, honey," Pike Naylor said encouragingly, "because this'll be your home for a spell, I reckon. Unless you let her run away from you, Shanks."

Shanks turned and surveyed the girl from head to foot with an increasing sneer of disapproval.

"She ain't gonna run farther'n hobbles will let her," she said. "She's gonna be right still and quiet in this here house of mine, because I don't hanker to be disturbed none. What's the game with you, Pike?"

"You keep her," Naylor said. "Keep her for a month, and I might be back for her. Anyways, keep her for a month. I'm gonna be mighty liberal with you, Shanks. Here's ten dollars to begin. Ten more if she's here when thirty days is up."

"She'll be here, alive or dead," Shanks assured him. "But not for no twenty dollars. Am I gonna board and lodge and keep a useless thing like her, I wanna know, for a whole month, at twenty dollars?"

"Whatcha want?" asked Pike. "What's the regular rate you charge for boarders out here?"

"I'll have fifty or nothin'," Shanks answered firmly.

"I've give you thirty," said Naylor.

Shanks nodded with a grin, as though this were more of a bargain than she actually had hoped to make.

"I'll keep her for that," she said.

"And keep her safe," said Naylor. "I don't want her starved, and I don't want her lost. Mostly, I don't want her lost."

"If she runs once, she ain't gonna run twice," Shanks assured him, measuring the girl, as if for a blow.

"They's a change of air comin'. I think a sandstorm is blowin' up," declared Pike Naylor. "I gotta be goin' back to the boys. Now, mind you, I'm gonna tell you what she'll tell you after I go. Have you heard tell of Geraldi?"

"Have I heard of the sun and the moon?" asked Shanks. "I've heard of him."

"He might want her. He might even come for her."

Shanks, with a scowl, stepped back and laid her great hand instinctively upon the barrel of the long rifle.

"Aye," old Pike said, "if you was to count him out of the game, they'd be more than thirty dollars in it for you. They'd be three hundred!"

Shanks grinned and nodded, her shaggy red hair flopping about her face. She made such a picture of ugliness as Mary had hardly dreamed of before that moment. She was as huge as a man. The sleeves of her flannel shirt, rolled up to the elbow, revealed forearms streaked with long muscles, like those of an athletic man. Her shoulders were man-like, also, in their bulk; her feet were enclosed in great cowhide boots. But no summing up of details could present an adequate picture of her repulsive ugliness. She was unique, and all the more fearful because in spite of her great height and weight she was unmistakably a woman.

"Is that all you got to tell me about her?" she asked at last.

"That's all. Watch her like she was your right eye. Watch her like she was your right hand, too. They's one other thing that I wanna tell you before I go."

"Aye?" said the woman.

Pike Naylor came a little closer to her.

"I heard the other day about a gent that just got turned out of the hoosegow in Chihuahua . . . fine upstandin' gent with a cast in his left eye and a scar down the middle of his chin. I ain't namin' no names. I ain't tellin' you except what I've heard. But it sounds to me mighty like him. He'll be up here for you, Shanks, one of these here days."

"You lie," Shanks said, her voice calm but her eyes rolling wildly. "You lie, and the rest of 'em lie, always bringin' me good news, year after year, because no dirty greaser jail ever could've held Danny Bane for a single night . . . and he'd come back to me here faster'n a bird could fly, I reckon. You lie, but your lies don't mean nothin' to me. Get out, now, and leave me be. And curse you and the yarns that you fetch up to me."

Naylor waved a hand toward her, as though he did not care to argue about the truth of what he had told her, then he turned to the girl his wolfish, narrow face.

"Stay put and stay quiet," he told her, "and there ain't gonna be harm or trouble for you. Start any ructions and there ain't gonna be any holding back of Shanks."

He glanced toward the latter, and, seeing that she had turned away, he tapped his forehead significantly and shook his head, as much as to say that Shanks was a maniac whom it would be wildly foolish to rouse. Then he passed out from the shack into the darkness, and the girl heard the creak of the stirrup leather as he raised himself into the saddle.

Big Shanks followed one pace from the

doorway into the night.

"Hey, Pike!" she called.

"Aye, Shanks . . . what is it?"

"That what you told me, you liar . . . that what you heard about the gent in Chihuahua, d'you mean it?"

"I meant it. Cross my heart to die I meant it, Shanks!"

"G'wan with you!" she exclaimed. "I don't believe no word of what you tell. You was born lyin', and you'll die the same way."

Nevertheless, in spite of this expression of skepticism, she remained for an instant hanging in the doorway, while Pike Naylor rode away into the night, leading the girl's horse with him.

The sound of the two sets of hoofs, muffled as they were, made poor Mary Ingall feel that she was indeed cut off; for even if she could go in the right direction, she would not dare to venture on such a stretch of desert sands as they had ridden over in the three hours from the town.

Then Shanks swung around on her with a grunt.

"So," she said, striding slowly to Mary, "I'm gonna be troubled with you for a month, am I? Mind you, beauty, that I ain't gonna be really bothered twice. And the first wrong step that you make, I'll split your head like dry wood for you. D'you hear me? Shanks don't promise for nothin' when she talks!"

She picked up the heavy axe as she spoke, and it trembled in the grip of her strong right hand, while the muscles of the forearm leaped and knotted under the strain.

"Now," she continued, "we'll see that you ain't too free to worry yourself with wrong ideas."

She took from the wall what must once have been a chain from a trap. It was rusted, but not deeply enough to spoil the strength of the links. At each end of the chain were strong shackles. Homemade handcuffs, they appeared to be.

These she fastened upon the ankles of Mary, and then untied the cord that held her elbows together. As she did so, she laid her large grip upon the arm of Mary and worked her fingertips deep into the flesh.

"Flabby!" Shanks announced. "Flabby and soft as butter! Sleek, fat, and no good for nothing. But you're the kind that the men lose their heads over. You're the kind that they rage about and rave about and stay prayin' for. Heaven knows that I seen your kind before, and never no good in none of 'em. No strength in your hands, no strength in your heart, nothin' but smiles and whines. But that's what men fall for. Bah!"

She barked her denunciation in the very face of Mary, and the girl endured it in silence. She was not afraid of insults. She was afraid for her very life.

"Mind you," went on Shanks, "here I've got you, and here I'll keep you. And the first move that you make to get clear, maybe you'll get loose from the house, maybe you'll streak away for a while down the draw or over the hills, and straight across the sand . . . if you're that much dolt! But, when I foller you, I'll foller with the axe, and, when I catch you, I'll finish off your runnin' days at one lick!"

She took Mary by the shoulder and flung her away, like a useless thing for which she could only sufficiently express her disdain through some physical action.

Mary staggered with a sharp rattling of chains until she brought up with a crash against the wall. Still she did not speak, but stared, fascinated with horror and fear at the convulsed face of the giantess.

The latter grew suddenly thoughtful, muttering aloud: "But supposin' that Danny Bane was to come, after all . . . what would he see in you? Would he have the sense, now, to see what you are? Would he, now?"

# IX

## "SANDSTORM"

That which had come to light to Geraldi was the memory of Sam Grey. For if Sam Grey had been bought up by the enemy, it was hardly probable that Pike Naylor would simply keep him like a neutral around the town. Men like Sam, who carried their worth written in their faces and in their entire bearing, were hardly to be bought unless they were violently used, and Geraldi could easily guess what that use would be.

He was a desert man, the desert lay south, and one of Naylor's possible routes home lay across the sands. What more likely, then, than that Naylor had hired Sam Grey as a guide across the barren land?

All of this Geraldi speculated upon in flashes, as a man will do when his thoughts are swiftly on the move, and, at last, he was sure that he was right. So he had started eagerly away from the town, as Emily Ingall had been able to see.

He did not allow the speed of the black

horse to endure very long. It was not his purpose to burn up that fine animal with a single burst of sprinting, but once beyond the town he settled the stallion down to a steady jog-trot.

The sand washed about the hoofs of the black. Sometimes bits of dead, fallen branches from the brush crackled beneath them with a muffled sound, but otherwise they were away in the waste like a ship in the sea. Never was the smell and the sight of the sea dearer to a sailor than was this of the desert to Geraldi.

Behind him the town was a dimly glowing point, then nothing. The more detached he was from other men, the more he felt himself shrinking in importance. For desert travelers may be happy and proud among their fellows in town or village, but once on the broad plains they learn humility quickly. As for Geraldi, this was new country to him, the same as an uncharted sea to a seaman. His provisions were salt and a package of hardtack; his water tank was a single large canteen; his wind and sails consisted of the horse he rode, and that was perishable flesh. As for his ports of call, they were the water holes dotted at random here and there among the sands. It might be that he could cruise to them by following the trails of animals; it might be that he would miss them entirely. But at any rate, the desert was a trap as surely as ever the ocean was.

Even for its peril he loved it, and for the sense of nakedness that it impressed upon his soul. Men who have been partners on such an expedition keep for one another an abiding affection; even a horse grows to seem more than a horse; there is hardly a desert rat that will not talk to a long-eared, willful burro as though it possessed human intelligence to understand his words.

The moon rose. Its appearance helped him to change his course a little to the left in order to bear more truly south in the direction that he suspected that Pike Naylor would follow. And it was shortly after this that, looking behind him, it seemed to Geraldi that he distinguished forms moving down his trail. He was not sure for some time, but eventually he made out six figures working across the plain toward him.

He did not wait for them. No wise man will wait for strangers who are out on the desert in force. Calling to the stallion, he put forward at a lope again for several minutes, until the figures had disappeared in the moon mist behind him.

That moon rose higher, and the stallion had been working forward for several miles when Geraldi chanced to look behind him again, and once more he was assured that the cluster of figures was coming steadily on toward him.

They could not be walking. They were runners, and he wondered what earthly purpose they could have in trekking out across such a heartless plain as this? One thing he must do at once, and that was to discover if they were making for some destination of their own, or if they were really trailing him.

Again he put the black horse into his long-striding canter, and, dipping into a draw, he followed it a mile to the right, then struck off south once more. He kept up the canter for a good half hour, until the horse was breathing hard from the labor that the soft going made. Then he drew rein.

Although his mount stepped out with a will even when walking, in a short time, as he scanned the lower undulations behind him, he was aware of the same cluster of men moving toward him.

That settled all doubts. They were actually trailing him across the desert, even as he hoped to strike and stick to the trail of Pike Naylor. He was both hunter and hunted!

At this he rubbed his hand along his sleek, muscular neck of the stallion. The stallion had been able to carry the weight of Lord Winchelmere in the old days tirelessly and successfully; would it be possible for men to run him down when so light a burden as Geraldi was on his back?

No wonder that Geraldi laughed pleasantly beneath the moon at such an impossible chance.

Off he sent the stallion again, rather irritated that he had not straightened the good horse out for a steady gallop long before, to shake off these unknown enemies. As it was, his flight had resembled that of a rabbit, which runs until it no longer sees the enemy, and then squats to take breath and lets the hounds come up on its traces.

The air had grown hot and still now, and out of the south a rapidly mounting mist began to shut out the stars. Presently an acrid odor of dust filled the air; the eyes of Geraldi began to smart. He knew that the sandstorm was coming. So he tied his bandanna over his nose and mouth, cursing his bad fortune, and pulled his hat low over his eyes.

Then the wind came.

It was a long, sighing breath that rose out of the ground at first, but rapidly it settled into a gale of great force, blinding thick with the fine sand that it carried. He faced it for a scant few minutes, then knew he would have to halt.

He dismounted and made the trained horse lie down with its back to the cutting force of the wind. To the leeward of that barrier he himself stretched out, already choking from the lack of good air.

With his head sheltered in his arms as he lay, he had to breathe through the bandanna to strain the air to some degree of purity, but even the closely woven filter was not sufficient. Blown sand is of all things the most impalpable. It is this that hangs in thin clouds above the desert and gives to the desert sky its peculiar color. Now it was forced into the lungs of Geraldi, and into his nostrils, until he was gasping and exhausted, like a man swimming underwater.

Men have been known to die in such circumstances, not from suffocation, but from the fear of suffocation, which eventually forces them to tear off the muffler from nose and mouth and breathe of the sand-laden air without that filter. The result is quick stifling.

But Geraldi had been through such moments as this before, although perhaps none was so bad as this. The wind blew with increasing, indescribable force. As a stone gathers way, leaping down a long mountainside, so that wind gained force as it rushed over the wide, level expanse of the plain to fill some partial vacuum in the northland. It screamed on its way; it stamped, and shook the ground; it laid hands upon Geraldi's living bulwark and made the heavy body of the stallion tremble in its grasp. Sometimes it shrieked high above them. Sometimes it poured down from the sky like a sand blast turned down out of a hose.

No matter how tightly he had bound the bandanna, it was impossible for him to keep the sand from working down his neck. It pressed at the tops of his riding boots, moreover, and drifted down to his toes. It entered his squinting or tight-closed eyes. It filled his ears with silt. And above all, it entered the very substance of the wind as a stain enters water.

Half stifled, he lay patiently, waiting the long minutes out until it seemed to him that there was a slight abatement in the pressure. Then he glanced up and saw that the moon was rushing backward down the sky, so swiftly did the transparent clouds pour past her face.

That sense of error was changed, and now it seemed to be plowing her way against an angry sky.

The gale ceased as suddenly as it had

begun. The wind died away. And although the air was still darkened and made stifling by hanging clouds of dust, Geraldi got the stallion up, mounted, and continued his way, unhappy with the grit in his boots, down his throat, in his eyes, and heavy in his lungs.

The air cleared more and more, however, and presently he could look back to a little distance and see a huddle of six forms leaving the moon haze and the shadow of the storm just behind him. They had started their march forward before he had. They were in close range, and showed instantly the purpose for which they had come. A rifle clanged. With an oath, Geraldi threw himself forward along the neck of the stallion as the bullet whirred above his head. He fired backward as he fled, but he could guess that all his shots flew wild.

Other bullets kissed the air about him, but the stallion was running like a startled wolf, and the firing ceased from behind as the indefinite moonlight quickly made all shooting simply guesswork.

After this Geraldi pressed the stallion to a good pace, and through the night he worked steadily to the scrub, with the bald mountains growing clearer and clearer before him.

He was in the foothills when, from a low eminence, he saw before him a confused jumble of shacks that ran up and down both sides of a narrow ravine. Wrecked and time-ruined houses were these, and he recognized at a glance one of those dead towns such as spot the West here and there, where mining booms have called a hasty population together and left it stranded after a short period of prosperity, looting surface deposits.

It might be that the fugitives had taken shelter for the remainder of the night in this place, but he doubted it greatly. It seemed hardly likely that Pike Naylor would stop with his party at so short a distance from the town from which he had started. Moreover, there was no sign of a light.

Determined on a little closer investigation, Geraldi started down the draw, but he had not gone far before a small form darted out of a shack on his right and fled into the brush — a skulking coyote, fleeing with incredible speed.

Geraldi drew rein. If one of these timid beasts was in the deserted town, it was hardly likely that any human being was already there. So he turned the head of the stallion down the rocky draw, and, coming to a point where it shelved out onto the level, he headed southward again at a good pace, still turning from time to time in the saddle to scan the ground behind him.

However, he saw no sign of the runners who had followed him so far, and this was an odd relief to him. Their pursuit had reminded him of the chase of a crow after a swift hawk; the very attempt had made it more absurd, and more blood chilling.

# X

## "FIVE COME RUNNING"

Straight southward toward the mountains, unconscious of the golden opportunity to which he had been so close, Geraldi rode on from Kimber Creek.

His canteen was now half empty, but, although he was starved with thirst, he made a halt in order to pour what remained of the liquid down the throat of the stallion. Then he went on again through a blank country of rocks and sand. Or, where there was vegetation, it was a sham and mockery, like the greasewood that lay thin as smoke along the hollows and the draws. Where it grew, it did not mean water. It meant only a faint suggestion of water far underground, which the long taproots found and drew little by little into the brush. There was much life, perhaps, but it was dry life. The sand-parched throat of Geraldi craved water with an increasing bitterness.

He had hopes for what he might find in the throat of the pass before him. It opened a slit in the wall of the mountains, but when he gained this door to the south, he felt only a hotter blast of wind pouring in from the wider desert beyond.

On the lip of the pass he looked back, but the moon had declined a great deal, and the air of the desert was still dim with the passing of the sandstorm, so that he could not look back for any distance. However, so far as he could see, there was no sign of the six who pursued him.

He had no doubt as to what they were, now. They were Indian runners. He knew that it was said of these men that some of them could accomplish a hundred miles between dark and dark. Of what horse could more be said? Moreover, they knew the lay of the land. They might be aware of short cuts. Already they had proved that they had bulldog tenacity, and teeth able to kill; he was not comforted by their bad aim; all shooting in the moonshine is uncertain.

As he sat his horse on the verge of the pass, he considered gravely whether or not he should give up his game. He had ridden very far. The stallion's edge of speed and strength was quite used up, so that any tough mustang in good condition should be able to outmatch him in all but a short race. The odds were terribly against him. Not only were there the men under Pike Naylor — sure to be the pick of the pack — but furthermore he had against him the six patient trailers who worked at his rear, ready as wolves to kill. A grim admiration rose in him once more as he thought of the ways and the devices of old Naylor.

That brief pause for thought did not make him turn back, however. Lack of water was the chief peril now, greater than the danger of guns because more sure, and he knew as little of the country before him as of that behind. So he struck on ahead with a feeling that he was attempting the impossible, but with that bulldog determination of a man who often has dared and rarely has failed.

The pass was like a man-made cut, flat-bottomed, the rocks sheering back at a gradual angle on either hand. In that pass there was not a single shrub, not a single cactus, for even that grisly vestige of desert life had been scoured away by the wind that whipped continually through the rocks.

Geraldi was glad to come out on the farther side.

Before him was a gradual descent for several miles, and, dismounting, he gave the stallion some relief by running down it on foot, the horse following at his heels.

Where the flat began once more, he looked back to the new face of the mountains, now behind him, and, swinging into the saddle, he jogged the black forward.

Light began in the east, then circled the horizon, fenced about with black summits, near and far. He was committed to a vast amphitheater in the midst of which, he could guess, he would have to play out a game of life and death against great odds. But still he went on. By this time, perhaps, the six runners must be in the throat of the pass, swinging forward with tireless step. Retreat was not cut off.

This desert beyond the first mountains was unlike that of the other side in that the ground was broken into many swells and undulations. From the tops of the mounds he could see to a considerable distance, only to be blanketed from all view in the next depression. But he did not scan the way before him so much as the way behind.

He knew what he would see, and eventually he saw it — the same closely packed group of men swinging steadily forward behind him as the rose of the morning succeeded the gray, and then the golden brilliance of the day commenced.

Geraldi tried the stallion in a canter. The good horse responded gamely, but it was plain that his heart was half gone. The storm, the long march over difficult, soft ground, the heat, the dryness of the air, and the lack of water had sapped his strength at its root. The instant Geraldi gave the word the black stumbled to a halt, and then went forward with dejected head, his ribs heaving violently.

Geraldi had known that the stallion was spent, but he was shocked to discover how far gone the animal was in fact. It made him set his teeth hard and slide the Winchester from its scabbard. He realized the futility of this at once, and slammed the weapon back home.

One man may trick or baffle six; he cannot beat six trained fighters!

Water was his need — for him and for the horse, also.

And then, as he topped a rise, he saw a blue eye watching him from the midst of black rocks, far away and beneath him.

He told himself that it was a mirage, of course, that it could not be real. But at that moment the stallion lifted its head and cleared its nostrils with a start. Its ears pricked, and it pressed forward with a sudden lurch against the bit.

Surely it had smelled in the distance the water that its master thought he had seen but hardly dared to hope that his eyes had told him truth.

It was far away, set like an azure jewel in the midst of a great lava field, covered with what looked like burned and charred stacks of hay, great knobs, rough protuberances, and whole fields of sharp cinders cast out of a furnace door a million years ago.

So Geraldi let the stallion canter down the slope, twisting here and there as they entered the confusion of the lava beds. But as he went, he remembered an old adage learned somewhere out of schoolbooks. The obvious thing is not always the thing to do. Water was their pressing need, their most cruel desire, but why pause to drink when death by bullets might follow immediately?

True, he might give the stallion a few swallows, fill his canteen, and try to press on, but the lava beds made the rudest sort of going, and men on foot would have a vast advantage. To gallop the black through these cinders would cut the horse's hoofs to pieces in ten strides. He had to pick his way gingerly, and even then at the cost of cut fetlocks.

Geraldi tried to swallow, but his dry tongue and his dry throat refused to act, and merely half choked him with the effort. Yet he turned straight aside out of his line, dragging the head of the stallion forcibly about. For once the good horse balked, his hoofs planted wide apart, and his head viciously hanging down.

Geraldi did not try either to whip or spur, but, jumping down from the saddle, he went forward, and the stallion reluctantly followed — away from the straight line toward the water that had seemed to them both like a promise sent from heaven.

It was out of sight now, but the quivering nostrils of the horse told him its exact location down the wind. Yet he followed the squared shoulders and the high head of his master as he never had failed to follow in the past. The will of the man dominated, and the horse prepared to die, in dumb surrender.

Between two kinds of black lava, Geraldi paused, threw the reins, and slipped back a little distance until he was lying in a nest of broken black fragments that shone like shattered glass and reflected even the early rays of the sun until they were soon furnace-hot. However, the place was a secure refuge, and he lay there patiently, enduring the glare of the light and the pressure of the heat, with the rifle ready beside him.

Light as their footfalls were, he heard

them before he saw the enemy come up from behind. The lava cinders turned and ground beneath their feet, and now the first man came into view, running steadily, straight up from the hips, but taking a good stride.

He was an Indian, his long hair bound back from his face with a red string that pressed deeply into his forehead. His high cheek bones glistened with sweat. The skin of his face was strained, drawn by long effort, yet his expression was one of patient resolution and of fierceness combined.

He looked to Geraldi as the albatross looks among birds — all air and wings, with little body to him, so great was the chest and so lean the loins of the Indian runner. But he carried strapped across his back a rifle. Its weight must have cost him an agony in the all-night run, but still he swayed forward with faultless natural style, making every swing of his arms help him along, and every inch of his legs count. Heel first his foot fell, but almost on the level, and toeing slightly in; despite the distance he had come, there was a springing lightness in his run.

He was blotted from sight by the next black hillock of rock, and behind him, running in his footprints, came another. Yet another and another pursued the first.

They were as alike as four peas in a pod, these first four runners, each with tight trousers, with heavy moccasins, with loose shirts beneath which the big lungs were laboring. Each seemed all sinew and air; their lightness suggested in every case the hollow bones of birds; each had the fierce and patient face in strange combination, and across the back of each was the strapped rifle.

There was victory in their very bearing. They seemed inexhaustible in strength as the wolf is inexhaustible, or the buzzard that floats for a fortnight over the hot peaks without food or drink to sustain it. They ran on the desert as an Englishman upon his native turf, and Geraldi admired them while he feared them.

But he had counted only four. Where were the others?

Presently another came, but although he was as tall, as well-made, as straight, yet he had not run as well. His mechanism was not faultless, like the others, it seemed, for he ran with his head strained to one side, his lips grinned back, and one of them cracked, so that a small stream of red had trickled down his chin and dried there.

He went out of view. The sixth man did not appear at all, and Geraldi knew that, whatever the future held, he had to count on only four instead of six against him. That made a different story. They were not a third less dangerous; four were not a tithe as terrible odds as the six had made.

# XI

## "WAS IT ALL IN VAIN?"

The half lost hope rose again in the breast of Geraldi when he saw the last of the Indians go by. The sixth man, he could guess, had fallen out somewhere on the long trail, and there was small wonder, since between day and day they had covered a hundred miles at least, and much of it was bitterly difficult footing to pass over.

It was no wonder that they had guessed that he was going on toward the blue coolness of the water. There, surely, even though they found him gone, they would pause a moment to drink before they resumed their search after him.

Geraldi waited no longer.

He did not mount the tired black horse, but, leading the stallion, he trudged out of the lava beds and into the sand beyond. Already the sun was high enough to burn with scorching power. It was blow sand through which he walked, sinking ankle-deep. White blow sand, as pure as ever glittered on any ocean beach. It was gathered in great steep-sided waves, with the wind-marks rippling over it. Now and again, but very rarely, he saw the top of some almost submerged shrub, or another stripped almost to the taproot as the treacherous soil had fallen away, but otherwise there was no sign of life here. Not even a coyote would have ventured willingly across this terrible desert, not even a big-footed jack rabbit would come here, except with dangerous enemies behind him.

But Geraldi faced the labor and the peril before him willingly. The sight of the set, strained faces of the Indians as they ran down the trail had convinced him that anything would be better than to confront them.

With this in mind, he faced the white waves of the sand, although still his throat was too dry for swallowing, and he had to repeat to himself over and over again a phrase that rang with a dull beat in his ears: *All things have an end! All things have an end!*

The white waves of the sand closed around him. He was shut out from all sight of living things, but forever he was slipping down steep, yielding slopes, and then laboring up the farther side, with the weary horse snorting and heaving behind him.

The glare was so terribly strong, as the sun rose higher, that the torment of his eyes was almost as great as the torment of his thirst, and then, climbing to the top of a small hollow, it seemed to Geraldi that his whole soul was plunged into an ecstasy. For all was green beneath his eye in that hollow — small shrubs and strong desert grasses, and in the heart of the hollow a spring welled up.

There was little religion in Geraldi, and yet now he could not help looking up with a quick smile, for it seemed as though divine kindness had brought him to this spot. When he looked up, the sun blazed back at him, and the light of it dazzled his eyes.

He went staggering down the slope and fell on his knees by the edge of the pool that formed beneath the little spout of water. He thrust his hands in deeply above the wrists, and drank, and raised his dizzy head, and drank again. Then, remembering that too much water after famine is not good, he filled his canteen and allowed the black horse to drink in turn.

The stallion plunged in his head almost to the eyes; and Geraldi smiled with dry, twitching lips as he saw the great bolts of water sliding one after another down the throat of the horse, and heard them gurgling audibly into its stomach.

So ended the starvation for water.

Geraldi crouched for a moment on his heels, chewing hardtack, regardful now of even such a small trouble as the heat of the sun between his shoulder blades. Then he stood up and took the eager horse from the water long before it had had its fill. With handfuls of clear water, then, he washed the eyes, the nostrils, the legs of the black, and dashed some up against its belly. After that he turned to leave the place, with the stallion behind him.

For it was barely possible that the Indians, who knew all things about the desert, might know of this place, also, and, having failed to find Geraldi at the big pool, they might come to this, instead, to shut him off from all supply.

So he hurried on.

The water from the little spring was not all soaked up in the pool by the porous sand that held it, but some trickled away down the narrow draw toward the south, and here the grass appeared, making a good footing, and the brush grew tall and strong. It would have been a commonplace in any other country; on the desert it was a true bit of heaven, and Geraldi and the horse both dreaded leaving it.

He wished to give the black still more time to recuperate, and for that reason he continued to lead it down the green trench, walking rapidly, and tugging the horse after him.

The way twisted here and there, as the water had slipped from stage to stage, winding its way out, diminishing in volume from place to place as the thirsty sands drank of it. Geraldi, rapidly rounding a corner, caught his foot under a root that was buried in the loose sand. The jerk pulled him forward, off balance. It would have downed another man, but Geraldi half recovered, merely touching the ground with one hand.

In that instant, however, he heard the familiar whistling of a lariat in the air. Floundering as he was, one hand went for his Colt as he tried to dodge to the side, but a shadow brushed past his eyes and a flexible, thin tentacle gripped him around the shoulders, jamming his elbows against his sides, stiffening his helpless arms.

Another lariat's noose dropped over him. In a trice he was bound from head to foot, and only then did the red men come out from the bush behind which they had been screening themselves.

Slowly they gathered around Geraldi,

their breasts still laboring from the long effort that they had made, their cheeks sunken with work, but their eyes cruelly bright with satisfaction. They had conquered, and at their feet lay the victim. He was helpless on his back, and the tallest and strongest of the four, reaching down, took him by the hair of the head and jerked him into a sitting posture.

This, however, was apparently not to the pleasure of another, who looked older, and spoke with authority a few sharp words to the offender. Whether it was respect for Geraldi that made him protest, or merely that he was reserving the captive for some ultimate purpose, Geraldi could not tell, but he felt a touch of hope at once.

Two of them, in the meantime, ran to catch the stallion, but a shrill whistle of warning from Geraldi startled the black horse away. It was an old signal that Geraldi had taught the horse long before. It meant, in the code that they had established between them: "Go home at once!" Having heard it, the stallion wheeled, floundering through the soft sand, and made off.

It was the last gesture of Geraldi to connect himself with the world that was left behind him. The Indians seemed to grasp the importance of the move at once. After all, a return horse is no great rarity in the West, and if the stallion reappeared in the town, it would be a sufficient warning that something had happened to the man who had ridden him out into the desert. Search parties would be started. And the black was quite capable of leading them back down the trail on which he had ridden. No wolf would be able to follow more perfectly the way that he had come out from the town, step by step, in all its windings. This hope was vague and dim in the mind of Geraldi, but better a small and faint light of hope than none at all.

As for the Indians, they unslung their rifles, shouting to one another, and he who seemed the leader actually got in a shot before the horse floundered over the first ridge out of view.

Whether he was hit or not, Geraldi could not guess, but the marksman seemed discontented. He yelled loudly, but he remained close by Geraldi while his companions ran forward to the ridge to shoot again.

In silent agony, Geraldi sat in the hot sand and listened and watched. But the Indians ran on, disappeared, and still their shots came ringing and echoing back among those naked dunes.

It was some moments before the shooting ended, still longer before the three came trooping back, and by the first glance at them Geraldi knew that they had failed, for as they came, they halted and glanced angrily back over their shoulders, then came on again. For that matter, it would have been no easy mark to hit the swift horse as he dipped up and down among the sand hills, now against the sky, and now dropping from sight altogether.

How long would it take him to go back? How much time would he spend stopping to graze, or to drink? For he was both hungry and thirsty still.

The four were now rejoined by the fifth, who perhaps had been attracted by the sound of the firing. He came staggering in, looking hardly fit to bear his own weight, but, when he saw Geraldi a helpless prisoner, he straightened up as though he had taken a strong stimulant.

The four argued swiftly, standing close together, now and then throwing keen glances toward Geraldi. The leader, however, did not join in the apparent debate, but broke into it with short, jolting words from time to time.

It was impossible for Geraldi to understand what the debate was about, except that the four pointed in one direction, and the leader kept indicating the south. His will finally prevailed. The others sullenly gathered twigs and branches from the shrubs that grew along the edge of the water-run.

These they heaped in four small piles, lighted them and, when the flames were strongly started, at the same moment placed upon each fire green grass and green leaves, so that presently four small, thick columns of smoke were rising straight and high into the windless air, to be visible for many a mile across the plain. It was the age-old Indian call to council.

They maintained the smokes for some time, all the while staring toward the south until, at a grunted order from the leader, the several fires were extinguished.

The reason seemed to be clear. When the fires were out, Geraldi clearly saw, far away in the south, a single dim streak of smoke that answered the first signal clearly enough by saying: "I am here." Or, in other words: "I am leaving this spot to come at once."

Who was it that would come?

That question was answered at once by the leader, who jabbed his moccasined foot into the ribs of the prisoner and pointed toward the distant smoke column with a malicious grin.

"You see?" he queried.

Geraldi nodded.

"Pike Naylor," said the Indian, and grinned again.

# XII

## "WHEN REAL MEN BLOOMED"

When that same morning came for Mary Ingall, it was the harsh, snarling voice of Shanks that roused her from sleep. She sat up in the bunk, and the rattle of the chain that gripped her ankles told her quickly and forcibly where she was. Day was hardly beginning, and, in the half light, Shanks looked more monstrous than ever.

"Get up," she said, "and hustle your shoes on. You're gonna start the day with a little work, baby face. Stamp into them shoes and then grab this bucket."

Mary Ingall, obeying, slipped on her shoes and picked up the four-gallon bucket that was kicked toward her.

Then she stepped out, shivering into the gray of the morning. The moon of the night before had failed to show the full wretchedness of the deserted mining town. The gloomy morning told all the story to the eyes of the girl, and she thought it more tragic than any tale she ever had heard. Wrecks, and tangles, and half-destroyed labyrinths of ruin, they looked as a doll's house looks, a village filled with dolls' houses, when some malicious boy has been allowed in to kick and batter all within his reach. So powerfully did this picture grow in her imagination that she almost saw how the great hands had fallen from above and crushed and wrenched and distorted.

Those who had lived within the shacks? Some perhaps succeeded in escaping, scurrying here and there like gophers for their holes. Others died in the ruins, their death screams going up to the ear of the destroyer no more loudly than the squeaking of mice under the housewife's broom.

So vivid had the fancy become that she had to shake her head and draw a short breath to expel the nonsense. It was only wind, weather, and time that had laid their hands upon the town and wrecked it. As for the men, few of them perhaps were living, for that matter. Guns, and knives, and wild living, and bucking horses, and thirsty deserts, and winter blizzards had picked them off one by one. After all, there was not so much error in the first picture of her mind.

It seemed to poor Mary Ingall that all life here on the desert was a thing of flux and change, appearing in a sudden flush like the short-lived flowers that make spring for a day and wither for another year at the first touch of true summer sun. Were there not dew flowers that it seemed the dew alone fed, which opened in the rose of the morning, and died as the sun went up the sky? So were men and women here upon the face of the desert, sometimes pouring out in numbers where gold appeared, or where it was hoped for, and then blotted up by the fierce, hot action of the desert life. Whisky dew was that on which many of them blossomed, and they were ruined and slain by the thing that nourished them.

These figures poured through the mind of the girl as she watched the houses drifting past her.

"What happened here?" she asked.

"Hey?" barked the big woman, turning on her.

"What happened to all the life in this town?"

"It went dead," said Shanks, her voice rough, but no rougher than usual. "It went dead, like everything goes in this here part of the world. The Kimber, it dried up. They turned it in the Kimber Hills, the skunks that was working the hydraulic mines up yonder. They used it up and turned it down the new valley, and never no more of it come down here. What happened? Why, what happens to a tree when you cut the taproot? That's what happened here, pretty face. What would happen to you or to me if our throats was cut. That's what happened to Kimber Creek, d'ye understand?"

"Yes," said Mary Ingall breathlessly. But she was glad to get the other talking; it seemed impossible to propitiate her in this fashion. "But that wasn't right. The water shouldn't have been taken away from the people here. There should have been a law, surely. . . ."

"Law? Hey, what're you talkin' about?" Shanks growled. "I'll tell you what . . . there wasn't no law in this part of the world in the days that I'm talkin' about. Thank goodness there was no law, and that was the time that the real men come and the real men bloomed. I seen the time you could walk down the street of Kimber Creek, here, and out of every ten that wore trousers, there was one that was a man, with his knuckles as hard as leather, and wildfire in his eyes and wildfire in his heart. Them was days when it was worth while bein' alive!"

Mary Ingall nodded. She had no words to answer this.

"Him . . . Geraldi," Shanks continued,

"he would've been allowed inside of the town, that's all, in them days. He would've been kind of a roustabout, a joke, compared to the real men, d'ye see? A water boy, a timekeeper, a dog-gone cook, compared to the real men of Kimber Creek. I seen, once, Hal Dennis, and Jimmy Fay, and Spooks Larson, and Danny Bane, all standin' in one spot, all talkin' together, all ready to kill, all about startin' for the draw, all. . . ."

She paused, and struck the bucket she carried with a crash against a broken end of board that stuck up out of the sand.

At this, a deer bounded into view from behind a house, straight toward them. Mid-leap it saw them, and made a frantic effort to double back. Had its feet been on the ground, perhaps it would have been able to dodge away, but as it landed, a long, blue-barreled Colt slid into the capacious hand of Shanks. She seemed, to Mary Ingall, in no hurry to fire. The deer had landed from his long bound and twisted about to flee when the woman fired, and the beautiful little animal crumpled on the ground and lay still, with eyes yet bright and wide open.

Shanks did not step toward the dead quarry at once. She remained for a moment with the revolver gripped in her extended hand.

"Men leaped up like that," she said, "in Kimber Creek. They come flashin' into town and sung their song, and they died like that. But their heads was broke before their hearts was broke. That was proper livin' . . . not to drag out a life like they do now, losin' their youngness, losin' their pride, losin' their manhood, and then only livin' because they fear death. Oh, them days was the real days, and them was the real men. Like Fay and Larson, and Paulding and Jenkins, and Danny Bane, the king of 'em all!"

She spoke this out in a tone half exultant and half bitter. Then she went to the deer and measured it with her eyes, cut its throat, and then marched on with red hands toward the water.

The girl, sick at heart, followed.

It did not seem like the killing of game, but rather like a murder to her, that sudden upstarting of life and beauty, and that sudden ending of it.

The water was a standing tank in a hollow among the sand hills just behind the dead town. It was a horrible thing to see, the edges being coated gray, purple, and green with dried scum, and all the surface of the water was marred by the same slime. Yet, here and there the deep hoof marks of cattle appeared, going down to the water's edge, some freshly made, and others anciently hardened to stone by the heat of the sun.

A step or two from the edge, Shanks, undismayed by the horror of the water, scooped out a pair of shallow holes.

"I'm gonna teach you how to make an Indian well," she said. "This'll be your job, after this. If I'm gonna do the cooking, you're gonna fetch the water for me. That's the least. There ain't gonna be no idle hands around my camp, baby face."

As the water seeped in from the tank to the hole, Shanks bailed it out twice. Finally it ran in as crystal clear as the water from any spring.

"It ain't as sweet," explained Shanks, "as mountain water or well water off the hills, but it won't harm you none. It's been sifted and filtered through four foot of sand and gravel and such, and it'll have no dirt in it. Fill up your bucket, and we'll start back, and don't forget the trick when you come back a second time. Dig a new hole, and bail it out twice. The third time turns the trick, and the water won't make you sick none at all."

Mary, with a sense of nausea that she had to fight off with a distinct effort of the will, followed the directions of Shanks, and started back with her toward the shack, her shoulder quickly aching from the dead weight of the four gallons of water.

They passed other houses, as they went, that looked both larger and in a far better state of repair than the one in which Shanks made her home. Mary could not help wondering aloud why it was that one of the deserted places had not been taken by her companion.

"That's a fool question," Shanks replied harshly. "Because that's where I lived when Danny Bane last seen me, and that's where he'll come back for me. Is he one to waste his time lookin' around if he don't find me the place where I said I'd wait? He ain't. He's got plenty on his mind besides me. Might be even when he come, he wouldn't take to me so strong. I never was no beauty, and I ain't even what I was, I reckon."

She turned a savage eye on her companion as though she dared her to speak, but Mary could not look into that grotesque mask of a face and speak a word of reply, nor one syllable of comfort.

"Howsomever," growled Shanks, "I ain't one to be left behind. When he comes back to me, he wouldn't dare to ride on without me. Not him! Nor would no man that ever give me his word, the sneakin' pack of liars!"

This oddly jumbled speech, together with

what she had heard the evening before, convinced Mary that her companion was a little more than half insane.

Here she waited in the wreck of the town of Kimber Creek for the return of her lover, he whom she had picked out in the old days from among the wild roisterers and fighting blades of the town. What had happened to him was not even to be guessed. But the greatest probability was that he had been dropped in some barroom brawl, as most of the "heroes" of the old days fell. Or a knife in the back might have ended him, or a bullet fired beneath the table as he tried crooked tricks at poker.

But here waited Shanks, growing older, more terrible, more insane from year to year, but still in one quality divine, for she had endless faith.

It made Mary Ingall humble of heart, for, as she looked around on the dismal face of Kimber Creek, she told herself that she would far rather die than remain here a single year for any stake. Death would be far more pleasant.

They reached the spot where the deer lay dead, and she was given the other bucket to carry on toward the shack, while Shanks remained behind to skin and butcher the deer. Mary, picking up the extra bucket, staggering under its weight, remembered that the rifle stood in the shack and that her hands would be free to grasp it!

# XIII

## "A KNIGHTLY HORSE"

In the cabin, she put down the heavy buckets and took up the rifle at once, but the moment it was in her hands, she knew that she lacked the courage to go ahead. She had seen a gun in the hand of Shanks and knew how straight that veteran could shoot. Rifle against revolver still did not make the odds right in her estimation, and when the loud, raucous voice of Shanks called for her, she put the rifle back in place and went out to assist in the skinning of the deer, holding here and pulling there, according to the directions of Shanks, who lifted off the pelt with the speed and the skill of an Indian hunter. Then she butchered the game with equal speed, and bore the spoils back to the cabin.

She did not use the stove for this cookery, but established an open fire before the cabin, with Mary hobbling in her chain here and there to pick up wood and maintain the blaze. Above the fire, suspended by a pot-hanger and a wire, hung a choice cut of the venison, which was made to turn and return regularly by a fan of wood, twisted into the wire. Like a sentient thing, the venison twisted back and forth above the blaze, hissing, and snapping, and gradually roasting a rich brown.

It was slow work, and not until the middle of the hot morning did they breakfast. It was close to noon before they finished the meal and the cleaning up of the fire and the tin plates. Shanks, with that, announced her intention of sleeping for an hour, and invited Mary to do the same.

She gave quiet advice: "There ain't any use in you hangin' around with a scared look all the time, baby face," she said. "I ain't gonna wring your neck, I reckon, unless you start cuttin' up. Lay down and sleep, and it'll freshen you up for the fag end of the day. But if you want, you can go and take a walk, and start wishin' that you was free, and sighin' and groanin' off by yourself. Only, don't you go past the end of the town, and stay close enough for me to fetch you with a holler, because if I have to start runnin' to bring you in, you're gonna have something happen to you that'll make you tolerable sick the rest of your days."

With that, the bunk groaned as she stretched her formidable weight upon it, but

Mary Ingall took the second alternative, and dragged her hobbling chain out through the doorway and down the narrow ravine of Kimber Creek through the baking white heat of the noonday sun.

It was as melancholy a walk as ever a mortal could take, among the wrecked shanties of Kimber Creek, and, when she was below them, with the bare, hot rock of the draw before her, she paused again, and sat down in the shade of an overhanging boulder, looking north from which help would come.

But no human help would come, she knew. Geraldi, for all his cleverness, would not be able to find his way past the desert, with the marks of the early trail made by Naylor and the others now wiped out completely by the sandstorm. And if Geraldi could not come, how could any other get to her?

There was no hope. The league of the hot, white sand and the smoky desert shrubs closed her in as effectually as ever the ocean shut in a stranded mariner on a desert island.

She fell to watching the progress of the steep shadow, as it crept in under the rock, and at last reached her feet. Already her shelter had become too hot to endure, and she had made up her mind to move, when the raucous voice of Shanks bellowed in the distance, calling after her.

The hour was ended, it appeared, or else Shanks's nap had been broken. So Mary rose and stepped out into the furnace flare of the sun. It was so powerful that it pierced at once through her coat and shirt, and burned the skin of her shoulders, and it scorched her hands, and the unflung reflection of its power stung the skin about her eyes.

There was a sharp clanging sound of iron on rock that made her look down the draw, and there she saw a thing that made her cold in spite of the summer heat about her. It was the black stallion of Geraldi, crossing the rock at the mouth of the draw, and then pausing on the farther side to graze for a moment on the grass that sprouted at the base of a sand bank.

Geraldi's horse, and with an empty saddle!

She called out, and ran toward him as fast as her hobbled feet permitted, but the horse swerved away at the sound of the chains.

In an instant he was out of sight.

So would a sailor have felt, if the chance boat washed on his shore had been drawn away again in the waves — so would he have felt as Mary felt then.

And behind her the great voice of Shanks rose and boomed faintly upon the air, with a distinct note of anger in it now.

She turned and hallooed in answer, hoping that would quiet the watchful dragon. Then she sent after the stallion the whistle that she had heard Geraldi so often use to call the horse.

He came at once, standing above the nearest dune of sand, and, looking down at her as she approached, his head canted to one side in a very human attitude of inquiry.

Again she whistled, and this time the stallion tossed his high head, as much as to say there was something wrong with the whistler.

However, at the third call he plunged suddenly down the bank and stood before her.

She came toward him with both hands outstretched, speaking softly, while the nervous stallion drew cautiously back, watching her with bright, suspicious eyes, and sniffing toward her hands his hot breath. He knew her well, but she was not his master.

Behind the girl the voice of Shanks came again, this time dimly dissoluble into words: "D'you hear me, hey? Come on in! Where are you? You baby face, I'm gonna give you a lesson. . . ."

The rage of Shanks increased at this point until her voice became a screeching blur.

And the stallion, hearing that distant threat, danced farther off, the broken reins dangling from his head.

Despair came upon Mary Ingall, and such an overmastering fear as she never had known before. She dreaded more than any man the big, powerful cruel hands of Shanks. There would be no mercy in the hands of that woman.

Once more she tried the whistle, despairing of success, but still faintly hopeful.

This time the stallion came straight to her, shaking his head exactly like a man in doubt, but compelled above his own will by the well-remembered sound of that command. In another instant she had the reins, and had knotted the ends of them together.

But how to mount? The stirrup was high, the horse distinctly nervous, and her feet were bound together with chains!

She caught the pommel and the cantle of the saddle, but as she strove to drag herself up, the big horse side-stepped, and she almost fell. At this, he reared back, standing straight up on his hind legs and looking as though he were going to strike her to the ground.

Better that than to fall into the hands of Shanks, whose voice now thundered close at hand.

She went straight in, fearlessly in, and the threatening bulk dropped harmlessly to the ground, yet with a *clank* of the armed hoofs against the rock that could not fail to reach the ears of Shanks! Would it be a sufficient alarm to start her running toward the spot?

It was, for now she heard Shanks crying out again, her voice shaken by the effort of running.

Dragging the stallion to the side of the draw, Mary tried to climb up on the side of the sandy bank. It crumbled beneath her, and, as she slipped down, she saw Shanks come around the nearest corner of the draw.

A wild yell came from that terrible woman as she saw the scene that was being enacted before her. The cry made the black horse shrink back, stiff with surprise, ready to leap away. As he shrank, Mary tried for the saddle the third time.

Fear itself gave her the extra lift, the spring in her legs, and the power in her arms, to draw her up. She lay like a log across the saddle as the black horse shot down the draw in fear.

At any moment she might be jolted off, but she looked back toward Shanks, in whose hand the long, straight-shooting revolver now appeared, not leisurely, as she had seemed to do in firing at the deer, but with a flashing speed.

The gun spoke. So tense was the gaze of the girl that she saw the muzzle of the gun jerk up as the cartridge exploded. A bullet went past her with an angry, brief note of music.

Another, another. . . .

And like magic a sandy shoulder of the lower draw sprang in between the marksman and her quarry!

The great speed of the black horse had accomplished this much so suddenly, and, veering out of the depression, he cantered on across the open for the distant town.

She let him run for a full half mile, without daring to change her position, but at last she drew him back to a walk, and then set about righting herself in the saddle.

It was not easy.

She had been raised to ride astride, but now, with her fast-bound feet, she must strive to manage aside. So she struggled upright, then turned, and managed to hook her right knee over the high pommel of the range saddle.

It was a most uncomfortable and precarious position. For her left foot did not reach down to the stirrup, which could not be shortened enough to accommodate it. So closely did the chain hold her ankles together. She had to remain there, sadly twisted, and grip the pommel with one hand, the cantle of the saddle with the other. As for the reins, she kept them tucked under her arm.

So, looking back, she saw Shanks running frantically in pursuit, the useless revolver flashing in her hand, her voice blowing faintly down the wind like the scream of a hungry eagle as it stands on a tower of crag.

It seemed to the girl, as she dismissed the danger of Shanks from her mind and concentrated upon the problem of Geraldi, that the horse must be going in the wrong direction. His master was in some trouble, some danger, and the black horse had started home, for she knew that he was a return horse of rare quality. It was not that way she wished to go. It was back toward the spot where Geraldi had parted with the stallion — under what circumstances she dreaded to think.

So she turned the good horse about. Twice he veered back with a lurch and a snort of anger, but finally she persuaded

133

him, and like a sulky child, with hanging head, he faced about toward the mountains, and the narrow throat of a distant pass.

# XIV

## "NO HELP WITHIN FIFTY MILES"

In the narrow pass of rock, in the late afternoon, the strength of Mary Ingall gave way, and she decided that she could not endure her cramped position any longer. Whether she would be able to mount the stallion again or not, she had to dismount, and this she did.

It was a marvelous relief to walk up and down and stretch her cramped legs. In the shadow of the rock she lay down, and the throbbing ache in her back gradually subsided. Then she sat up to consider further possibilities.

The black horse stood, too utterly fagged to pay heed to food, if food there had been nearby. His head hung down, his eyes were dull, but yet by the steadiness that he had shown in following one course, Mary was reasonably sure that this was the line that Geraldi had taken in coming away from the town.

How to continue along that trail she could not tell, for it was a nightmare to get again into the cramped position which she had been occupying before.

She considered the iron that held her. The bands that were clamped around her legs were by no means new, but she understood that the lock would hardly give to her skill or strength. The chain itself might be a different matter.

It had evidently been at one time part of a trap, and, although the links were large enough to have held either man or beast, still it seemed to her that they might be sprung wide enough by hammering to undo them at the point where they fastened to the shack rings themselves.

She set about it at once. On an edge of stone she placed the key link from her right ankle and pounded it strongly with a fragment of loose rock. The first rock crumbled. With the second one she made a mis-stroke that clenched the link more firmly than ever and cruelly bruised her leg.

But still she kept at her work.

She tried the left foot shackle, since the right one seemed to be too tough for her, and at the very first stroke the link gave and spread a little. At the second, it not only gave but actually cracked.

Her heart leaped, and the next blow had made her almost as good as free.

There was still the shackle iron itself around the left leg, and the iron and the chain suspended from her right ankle, but she was free to move as well as she could, with those encumbrances.

The chain was disposed of without difficulty by tying it at her knee with a saddle thong, and she was able to mount into the saddle, after shortening the stirrups, and ride at ease.

She felt twice the command over her horse, now; she could ride forever, she felt, but the burden of worry was on the horse. Long and swiftly had he traveled since he first left the town with Geraldi in the saddle on his back, and now he was reduced to a plodding thing, like a broken-down work horse.

However, he was both burden-bearer and guide, and she had to force him on, although it made her pinch her lips at the cruelty of such torment. Steadily he went on, with a measured and sometimes a fumbling step, and so they came at last to the end of the pass and started down the easy pitch of the slope beyond.

She saw the water first, among the lava beds, and, going to it, both she and the stallion partook of new life. But when she mounted once more, she was surprised to see that the wise horse turned aside at right angles to his former course, and led on into blow sand, piled in stiff white waves, marked by the restless fingers of the wind with many patterns.

Her bewilderment turned to an odd mixture of astonishment and alarm when she saw before her, floating above the tops of the dunes in the rose of the sunset, a single stroke of silver smoke.

It grew at once in volume, a liberal puff arising, and then a strong steady column that faded from view, or became obscure, as the light of the day faded into dusk.

She was about to turn the stallion around and flee, at first, feeling that there could be no friend in this place, even if the black horse had led her here. And then it occurred to her that Geraldi, perhaps thrown and hurt, might be lying here among the dunes into which he had gone — heaven alone could tell for what reason. But he had collected some wood and was making himself a fire — for cookery, perhaps, or even for the purpose of signaling.

This spurred her on, but she was too cautious to take the horse with her, lest he should reveal their coming by the noise he made in crossing the uncertain ground, or by the size of his silhouette against the sky as he loomed on a dune top.

She threw the reins, instead, and left the black horse standing, while she went on cautiously, but not before, with rare presence of mind, slipping from the saddle the sheathed knife that Geraldi — master manipulator of knives — always carried there.

Mounting every crisp white wave of sand, she approached the crest with consummate care, and peered over at all the horizon about her, and probed every hollow so far as her eyes could reach. Then she crawled down the farther side, taking care to choose easy descents down which she could pass without sliding noisily.

She worked on almost like a swimmer — and then her ear was struck and she was stopped by the sound of human voices, murmuring in the distance. Immediately on the heels of this rang harsh, strident laughter.

From this point on she went softly as a shadow. When a louder voice broke out, she winced against the ground. When the murmurs were more subdued, she crawled on once more, and so she came to the last ridge of all and looked down upon the shallow little hollow where the spring worked up in the center and around which grew the ranges of shrubs and the scattering of grass.

Beside the runlet of water shone the light of a small fire, and around this were gathered seven or eight white men, with Indians in the background, working to fetch and carry firewood, and laboring over cookery. There were three of these, and still farther back appeared a small host of horses, their saddles removed, except for three or four kept in readiness for a quick need, and the animals allowed to graze on hobbles.

Of the faces of the men, only two could she distinguish with any certainty. One was that of Pike Naylor, marked as it was by the white giant's beard which he wore, and the other was that of a man sitting close to the fire, with the light flickering over him, the center of attention from all the rest.

Geraldi!

His feet were bound together; his hands were lashed behind his back, which rested against the tough branches of a shrub, and in this fashion he leaned back as though at ease, and smiled upon those who were around him.

But Mary Ingall, seeing Naylor and the others, knew as clearly as though it had been called aloud at her ear that the very life of the prisoner was in peril. But still he smiled and chatted with the others about him, turning his gaily indifferent eyes upon them

140

one by one. All her heart went out to him in a great surge, and something opened in her very soul, as the lips of a singer part for music.

Out of her great love for him it seemed to her that she saw clearly what she must try to do. Down below the edge of the upper dune she must crawl, and, coming behind the brush, she must wriggle through, silent as a snake, until she was behind the place where Geraldi sat laughing among his enemies. If she could reach through to him, one slash of the knife would sever the ropes that held his hands together. Then, by passing the knife through, she would arm those dexterous, swift hands of his to slash the cords from his legs and enable him to move in his own self-defense.

She dared not wait to consider the many dangerous chances and possibilities that surrounded her, or what would happen to her if she fell again into the hands of Pike Naylor. These considerations she pushed behind her and started to work immediately, for fear lest her resolution might grow cold. So she skirted the rim of the dune and started over the top.

Exposed now on the inner side of the slope, it seemed to the frightened girl that the light from the small fire beat upon her as clearly as the light of the sun itself; she dared not glance down at the circle around the fire, but, hearing a silence and then a burst of chattering and rapid laughter, she told herself that they had pointed out her creeping form to one another, and then burst into a gale of laughter at her folly and at her temerity.

She looked up now, but only to see that many heads were drawn close together above the fire, where cookery was in progress.

The voice of Pike Naylor was next raised, and several of the Indians went scouring off across the sand, but she felt greater courage now, for she was lodged among the brush.

It was difficult work to get forward through this without making a great crackling noise, but she managed to do it, largely by taking advantage of the moments when there were many noisy voices around the fire. So she came up behind the very bush against which Geraldi leaned, with old Pike Naylor now beside him.

By the least turn of his head, it seemed to the girl, Naylor's old hawk eyes would glance back through the thin screen of the brush and perceive her. She flattened herself against the ground, hardly daring to breathe.

Then she heard the subdued whine of Naylor speaking.

"If you was to tell me about the rest of 'em, son, it would be all right. There's that boy of mine that went wrong and turned over to your side. I'd powerful like to get my hands on him. And there's Darcy that got away, with his crooked hands and all. You've let them drift on ahead, while you laid back and played to call us off their trail."

"And I succeeded in that, pretty well, as it seems to me," said Geraldi.

"You done pretty good," admitted Pike Naylor. "But we got you, at last, and here you are."

"Here I am," Geraldi said freely.

"It took the bait of a woman on the hook to get you out where we could nab you, and it took a good many hands on this side and that. But the main thing is that we got you at last, and here you set, and there ain't no hand within fifty mile that'll move to help you!"

"I don't know," replied Geraldi. "I'm not at all sure of that."

"You ain't?" said the other.

He started up on one knee, and, turning about, he glared back through the brush, and straight into the girl's eyes.

She lay still, not because she did not wish to leap up and run away, but because terror had frozen all power of movement out of her body.

# XV

## "YOUNG GENTS AND OLD IDEAS"

"You never can tell, Pike," said Geraldi. "I'll keep hoping till you have your knife in me . . . I'll keep hoping till you twist it in my heart."

"You talk like a fool," answered Pike Naylor. "But this is the thing I want out of you, Geraldi. Listen to me, because I ain't talkin' through my hat. Show me the trail that leads up to the other pair and I'll light out after 'em and take no more than what you took from me. D'you foller that?"

"That's what I hear you say."

"I'll do it, Geraldi. Sacred word of honor."

"You gave your word and your handshake to the girl."

The cackling laughter of Pike Naylor rose hideously in the night.

"Nobody's fool enough to take serious what's said to a woman. Not even the women themselves. You oughta know that, Geraldi."

"I took seriously what you said to her . . . or I wouldn't be here, Pike."

"It winds up at this," persisted Naylor. "If you'll tell me where to hunt down the other pair, then I'll turn you loose. If you won't, then they's a young and handsome life that ain't gonna see the light of the mornin'."

"I know nothing about them," Geraldi responded shortly.

The head of Pike Naylor began to bob back and forth.

"Young gents are full of old ideas . . . about bein' true to friends, and such stuff. But the fact is that there ain't many friends worth the truth, and you got only one chance in life to chuck away, Geraldi. If. . . ."

His voice was covered by an outbreak of excitement in the group cooking around the fire, and old Pike Naylor stood up to look into the cause of the noise.

Then, into the glow of the fire, came a man led by two of the Indians. He was blindfolded, his hands tied behind him, and to the rear came his horse, led by the reins. His face was bright red, like that of one who lives indoors and has been suddenly exposed to the brightness of the sun for a cruel length of time.

"It's Michaels," said a voice. "He runs the

pawnshop back in town . . . a regular land-shark!"

Another demanded: "What brought you out here?"

"Gents," said Michaels, "I come out here tryin' to find a great friend of mine. When you hear his name, you're gonna be sorry that you grabbed me like this. He's Geraldi."

There was a loud whoop of derisive laughter at this, and under cover of the noise the girl reached the knife through the bush and slashed the ropes that fastened the hands of Geraldi behind his back. His elbows stretched apart. She could faintly see his hands working behind his back, and into them she passed the handle of the knife.

Her work was done. Now, what would Geraldi accomplish? What could he accomplish, against such a crowd?

The breathtaking nerve-strain made her tremble and then froze her as if with cold.

Michaels turned his blinded face rapidly from side to side, and exclaimed: "I must be crazy! Do I hear you gents laughin' at Geraldi?"

"Hey, old-timer," called one of the men to Pike Naylor, "what'll we do with this one? The boys found him headin' toward the dunes."

"Find out what he was intentionin'," Pike said, still on his feet, and chuckling a little at the distress of Michaels.

"I aimed to find Geraldi," said Michaels. "I had to find him. It was worth thousands of dollars to me to find him, d'ye see? So I come out and rode into the desert. Been ridin' off and on for two days, pretty much in torture all of the time. About sunset, I seen smoke from here, and come straight along. I reckoned that it might be Geraldi, or someone that could give me a word about him. But I ain't meant any harm to none of you. You have my word about that. I'm a law-abidin' man."

He was as eager for his life as he ever had been to make a transaction in his pawnshop, and yet there was no whine in his voice. He had an odd dignity and direct simplicity.

"He's law-abidin'," Pike Naylor announced. "And he looks straight. Take him back and turn him loose with his hoss, and tell him not to come back this here way, will you?"

At this moment Geraldi reached forward and sliced in two the ropes that bound his legs together.

He was free!

What would he do next?

He stood up like a shadow behind old

Pike Naylor, and, reaching to the side, he slid the long Colt out of its holster on the old man's right thigh.

She saw Pike grasp suddenly at the empty holster, then whirl, and, as he whirled, the barrel of the Colt rose and flicked down. It sounded to the girl like the *clang* of metal on rock. She felt sure that the very brains of the old man had been dashed out as he sank to the ground.

Yet he writhed as he lay, and by that she knew that she had been wrong. There was still life in the venomous old serpent.

"Pike!" called a voice from the fire. "What . . . ?"

Then another shouted with such an agony of fear and rage and horror that it made the blood leap in the veins of the girl: "Geraldi! Geraldi! He's loose! The fellow's loose!"

He had left the fallen form of Pike Naylor and shot away like a hawk on the wing, running with incredible speed straight for the tangle of horses beyond the fire.

He was already almost among the stock when he was spotted, and frightened, hasty hands jumped for guns. At the first alarm caused by the bringing in of Michaels, the whole party, with admirable discipline, had prepared for a rapid departure, and the horses had been brought into a knot and hobbled. It was toward this mass of horse-flesh that Geraldi now raced, although the course took him perilously near to the guns by the fire.

As he came close, he shouted a sudden war whoop worthy of an Indian, and fired two shots into the air.

The horses turned and bolted. Those in front were slow in starting, and those in the rear stood up on their hind legs and pawed furiously to get away from this shouting, shooting terror of a man.

Into that mêlée of wild animals Geraldi plunged, while the girl stood up stiffly, her arms frozen to her sides, her hands gripped hard.

Guns flared and spat behind him; men with weapons in their hands lurched after him, but instantly the horses spun about. Like a whirlpool they drew Geraldi into their seething mass, and it was as a panther leaps on a horse's back that she saw the shadowy form of Geraldi spring into the mad confusion and cling to the bare back of a mustang.

The whole crowd of horses went off in a roar and a rush, with Naylor's men and the excited Indians running after them futilely, waving their hands, shouting in rage and disgust, which only served to frighten the horses more.

Through this confusion cut the voice, or rather the yell, of Pike Naylor, shouting wildly to his men to cut the fugitive down at any cost.

Rifles began to spurt fire. She saw a stricken horse leap into the air like a deer that has felt its death wound, but there was no rider on the back of the animal. Another hurt mustang stopped and began to spin in circles. A third plunged headforemost and did not rise again, evidently shot through the brain. More bullets cut and raked the horses, so that there were repeated squeals of pain and fear. On the whole the firing merely served to increase the speed of the racing mob, and over the waves of the dunes they disappeared — one of them bearing the shadowy form of the rider still on its back.

He was saved!

However, that was only a partial gain unless she herself could escape, for if she were taken, she would be the lure to call that wild hawk again into peril.

She did not wait to see the end of the action. Here was enough of a blind to cover her, perhaps, as she stole off down the back trail, while the men of Naylor's party worked to get after the horses and surround most of them before they were stampeded too far.

She went back through the brush as fast as she could, and then up the sandy slope toward the crest of the dune. Behind her, the fire struck some fresh, oily fuel and flared high, so that she flattened herself suddenly against the sand and glanced back in terror.

But all the men were gone south after the horse herd, and she only saw the tall form of Pike Naylor between her and the fire, his long, skinny arms thrown up toward the sky and his form looking black against the firelight, like a silhouette cut out of painted cardboard.

She went on, reassured, but when she gained the farther side of the low ridge and could stand erect, she found that her knees were trembling with weakness, and her heart was hammering so violently that she was half blinded, and her head spun.

She fought her way on through the loose sand and back to the hollow where she had left the black stallion.

He was still there with his thrown reins, but sufficiently rested to have his head up a little. He had drunk, he had rested, and sometimes rest is more than food. So when she clambered back to the saddle once more, he was willing enough to step out.

She, however, kept him at a walk, and put him straight on the back trail. Whatever reserve of strength he had must be saved for the final test, in case one of Naylor's men was quickly mounted and should happen to strike back to cut off Geraldi from the pass.

Geraldi himself she was still worried about. He had neither saddle nor bridle with which to control a half wild horse. Yet she trusted to his infinite resource to find a way out of the difficulty.

So she entered on the long slope up to the narrow mouth of the pass through the hills. There was no sign of Geraldi as she reached it. She passed through the double darkness of the night and the shadow in the throat of the pass, and, coming through on the other side, the stallion was still at a walk when she heard a horse's hoofs behind her, striking echoes from the steep walls.

Enemy, or Geraldi?

She turned, stupefied with excitement, and saw a rider on a racing horse come through. Then his shout split the air, tingling in her ears, and Mary Ingall swung the stallion about and raced beside him, laughing hysterically.

# XVI

## "WILL HE COME BACK?"

"In all of this," said Aunt Emily Ingall, "you will see for yourself, Jimmy, that luck has been overwhelmingly with you."

"Luck," Geraldi answered with his flashing smile, "is another name for what the hard worker gets. We've worked hard, Mary and I."

Mary, by the window, tried to smile in turn, but smiles came hard to her now. The terror of the long adventure was too recent.

"As a good, honest laboring man, then, Jimmy," went on the older woman, "you should see that you can't reap such large returns forever. We won't call it luck, then. But suppose Mary hadn't found the black horse?"

"She found him because he was a return horse, and was bound to go back past Kimber Creek. That wasn't luck."

"Suppose she hadn't been so alert, though, and hadn't chosen to walk out there by herself through the heat of the day?"

"That's what any high-spirited girl would have done. The cowards are the ones who stop hoping. She hoped, and so she kept moving. And that took her out of the hands of Shanks. It wasn't even coincidence."

"You're a convinced optimist, Jimmy. But look at Mary now! You can stand such things . . . do you think she can?"

Geraldi rose from his chair and went with his quick, soundless step across the room until he stood behind the girl and leaned over her.

"You're tired, Mary?" he asked.

"A little," she admitted.

"Aunt Emily," he continued, "thinks I'm going to carry you through one adventure after another, like this last one. She doesn't realize it's the end."

"Really the end?"

"Of course!"

"But," Aunt Emily said, "how can it be the end, when you still have what you took from Pike Naylor?"

Geraldi went to the table and, pulling open the drawer, he took from it the chamois sack that had seen so many hands. He had ripped it from the pocket of old Naylor as he felled him with the revolver stroke, unseen by the watching eye of the girl.

"Fair earnings," he said. "Simply fair winnings in this gamble."

"Will Pike rest content so long as you have it?"

"Are you suggesting," Geraldi asked, laughing, "that I should give it back freely to that murdering old vagabond?"

"Give it to charity, then," said Aunt Emily, "so that he'll know you haven't it still."

"Do you mean it?" asked Geraldi.

"Ask Mary."

Geraldi looked down with a frown at the girl.

"What do you say?" he asked curtly.

She closed her eyes.

"I don't want to say," she returned faintly. "I only know that so long as we have it, every time you pass through the door out of my sight, I think I'll never see you again."

Geraldi looked across at Aunt Emily, and that grim veteran nodded briskly at him.

"I understand, now," Geraldi said. "This must be the end. A man can't lead two lives. A married man can't."

"Of course not," said Aunt Emily. "A married man is simply an appurtenance of the home. I hope you understand that? That's why I never would have a husband. I pitied the poor creatures too heartily. But you can't be yourself and a husband at the same time, Jimmy. It's impossible."

Geraldi, without a word, took the chamois sack and placed it in Mary's hands.

"Pick out the charity," he said. "Only . . . don't let the charity have the name of Pike Naylor. I'll let you do anything . . . except buy off that old bloodhound. I go to sleep each night to sweet dreams of how he's growing starvation thin, yearning for his stolen treasure. Why, Mary, his nervous system extended to his money sacks, and, when I took them, it was worse than tearing out his heart. Let him die of it, but if you give the stuff away, then he'll have to transfer his hunt and everything but his hate to some savings bank or orphan asylum. Will it make you happier, dear?"

"Can you stand giving it up?" she asked him.

"Why," said Geraldi, laughing shortly, "I thought that it was our home I held in my hands, but it seems that it was no more than a bubble of danger and excitement. *Puff!* Away goes the bubble. But I'll make the home in another way."

He leaned and kissed the girl's forehead. Then, with a murmur of excuse, he walked out onto the hotel verandah and began to pace up and down.

Mary Ingall leaned forward, clutching the chamois bag to her breast.

"Do you think that it's the end?" she asked.

"What do you mean?"

"I mean, the end of his wild life?"

"You mean, the end of the old Geraldi, and the beginning of Mary's husband?"

"You can put it that way, if you want to."

"Ah, Mary, I can't tell. I wish that I could. I only know that to think of him settling down is a pitiful thing."

"But he loves me, Aunt Emily. And only last evening he talked beautifully about wanting a home and babies and all that sort of thing."

"Every pirate," Aunt Emily said, "loves to dream of lazy days in port and trembles to think of the rough sea . . . but that's where he drowns at last. That's a horrible way to put it, but I want you to know, honey, that the fight isn't over. At least not to my way of thinking. And, perhaps, as long as he lives you'll be in dread of the next day."

The girl drew a long breath.

"I'll trust Jimmy," she said almost fiercely.

"Heaven bless you, child, of course you will. And Jimmy will trust you, and try to trust himself as well. But in the finish?

Well, heaven take care of you both. There's only one thing that profoundly matters. You love one another, and you'll soon be married."

"Yes, we'll soon be married. What's that?"

"Nothing but a horse galloping in the pasture."

"It sounds. . . ."

She started up and went hastily to the window, drawing aside the curtain. So, with Aunt Emily beside her, she looked out across the barnyard and into the pasture to see that Geraldi was out there on the back of the black stallion, galloping him around and around the enclosure.

"Look at them go," said Mary. "How he rides . . . bareback or not makes no difference!"

"And see how the horse goes, with his head turned back, as if he were listening to Jimmy's voice."

"He is," said the girl. "He's listening . . . and I almost know what he's hearing, as well."

"Look!" said Aunt Emily.

As they watched, they saw the black horse take the fence in a long leap and rush far away through the open fields beyond, and so for a moment appearing against the skyline and dipping at last out of sight in a hollow.

At this, the girl turned with a start to the older woman and clung to her.

"He will come back?" she said.

"This time," murmured Aunt Emily. "This time, of course!"

# Smoking Guns

# I

## "PROLOGUE"

The rose of the dawn had hardly brightened into full day when Jimmy Geraldi came in sight of the cabin, and something about its face and the ruined clearing in which it sat arrested him.

He wanted breakfast, but not badly enough to hurry up to the door of this cabin before he had made a slight investigation and, as he sat on his roan horse in the dappling of shadows that fringed the clearing, his eyes began to brighten, for Geraldi loved all novelties, all dangers, as a cat loves delicate new cream.

He had ridden up from the ghost town that had once been the prosperous mining camp known as Saddle Creek. Its whole winding length of crumbling hotels, stores, houses, and shops could not now provide him with a single meal. Three bullets from his Winchester had bitten the heads off three squirrels, and their meat, roasted brown, was his supper. Then he had come on over the seat of Saddle Mountain, the center of the hollow between the cantle and the horn. It was a short cut that he had never taken before, and it led him to this clearing and its sense of destruction that had been newly wrought.

The cabin itself was a sturdy square-shouldered affair with one side badly scorched by the fire that had burned down a good-size barn or shed which adjoined. It was a very recent fire; the embers, here and there, had the sheen of black satin, and the ashes had not stopped blowing up like clouds of busy little insects.

There were a dozen or more pens and fenced corrals or pastures but, although the good condition of the fencing proved that they had been used recently, there was not a sign of horse, sheep, pig, or goat. Only one old cow, built like a boat of wide beam and shallow draft, stood patiently at pasture bars, waiting. The house seemed deserted, for, although this was breakfast time, not a wisp of smoke rose from the top of the chimney.

Looking closely, to detect some sign of life, Geraldi saw only the dark sides of the pine trees up the slope and the horn of Saddle Mountain, frosted white, high above them. While Geraldi watched, still making his observations like a patient beast of prey that knows only too well the trap and the gun of the hunter, an old man came out of the cabin door on a pair of crutches and went toward the pasture bars.

They were homemade crutches and too short for his shoulders. Moreover, he managed them with a strange, fumbling awkwardness. His left foot dragged crookedly on the ground while he hopped slowly along on the right leg.

When he came to the bars, the cow began to low, and, before he had dropped the last rail, it had jumped over and was running down to the rivulet of water that trickled in front of the cabin and gathered in a pool there. Into that pool the cow ambled shoulder-deep, and then, with closed eyes and ears laid back, it drank.

The old man at the pasture bars, in the meantime, looked after the cow with a crooked smile of understanding and pleasure. Then, without waiting to bar it again into the pasture, he started back for the cabin. He moved even more slowly than before, his white head bobbing up and down with effort. Halfway to the door he stepped on a loose rock that started him toppling. He made a few vague, floundering gestures, entangled himself with the crutches, and went down.

It seemed impossible that he could have hurt himself badly, but the bright, active eyes of Geraldi saw him lie without an effort during a long moment. When he rose, it was by degrees. He got to his knees, but the crutches he had to work with for a considerable time before he could stand erect, and resume his hobbling until he had disappeared through the door of the cabin.

The cow finished drinking, came out, and began to graze along the bank of the stream. And now it was that Geraldi left his post of observation and dismounted in front of the cabin.

Something was very wrong. He had felt it before, and he knew it now that he looked into the cabin, for the old man had slumped into a chair and sat with his head hanging and one hand dangling loosely toward the floor, the picture of one in the last stages of despair or exhaustion.

With two efforts he raised his head and looked into the face of Geraldi. He began to push himself up from the chair, exclaiming: "Why, hello, stranger! I'm glad to see a face. Come in here and sit down. I'll make you some coffee."

"Sit still," Geraldi commanded with a gesture that stopped argument. "I'll do the cooking."

He opened the stove. A fire was laid in it, and a touch of a match started it blazing. As the heat roared up the chimney, Geraldi asked: "Where's the bacon, partner?"

"Why, fact is that I ran out of bacon the other day," said the old man.

"The devil you did! That's hard luck. And I don't suppose that you've got any fresh meat around."

"Don't happen to have any. I'm mighty sorry," added the host.

It was a very neatly arranged cabin, and the kitchen corner of the main room was kept in perfect order, the pots and pans hanging well scoured against the wall on one side, while on the other side of the stove a set of shelves formed the pantry. On the top shelf, Geraldi found the coffee can. He began vainly rummaging through the others, asking: "Any bread made?"

"I don't think there is," said the other.

"All right. Where's the flour sack? I'll stir up a pone."

"The flour sack's around somewhere," said the host.

He was out of his chair now, moving vaguely, helplessly on his crutches. He did not seem to know where to go.

Geraldi, his brown face calm, his blue eyes cruelly aloof, watched the old fellow

167

with a sort of disdain.

"The fact is," he said suddenly, "you haven't got a scrap of anything to eat in the cabin."

The embarrassed glance of his host avoided him. "Don't seem hardly possible that I went and let myself run out!" he apologized.

Geraldi stepped close to him and saw that the skin beneath the eyes of that cadaverous face was a pale blue, like the stain that often appears in hard limestone or marble.

"Just how many days is it since you've had a mouthful to eat?" he asked.

"Me? How many days? Why, it ain't long. I must've just sorter run out. And. . . ."

He could not meet the grim eye of Geraldi, who abruptly turned and took heed of the two bunks that were built against the walls of the opposite corner of the room, the blankets carefully folded on top of them.

"You don't live here alone," said Geraldi, his back still turned.

"No, oh, no! My boy Sammy lives here with me. Maybe you know Sammy Wilkes. He's big enough and noisy enough to make himself known."

Old Wilkes laughed a little as he made this jest; his voice, however, was a trifle husky.

"Where is he?" asked Geraldi.

"Sammy? Oh, he's away, just now."

"How long away?"

"Just a spell."

"When is he coming back?"

"Well, sir, I guess that he won't be coming back, neither. I'll tell you what, partner. Right over the hill you'll pick up the trail to Turnersville. It ain't more'n three mile to the town, and you can get yourself a good breakfast there. I guess you'll find all the beefsteak and bacon, flapjacks and fried potatoes, even eggs, there. You can have a good square meal in Turnersville. I'll just stew you up a cup of coffee before you start. I'm mighty sorry that there ain't anything just this minute in the house."

Geraldi stood in the doorway, looking over the bright beauty of the mountains, far and near. He demanded sharply: "Where do you do your marketing?"

"Me? Why, down in Turnersville."

"How'll you get down there? On your crutches?"

"No, I'll ride the bay mare down and. . . ."

"I've seen no horse around here," Geraldi observed.

"Ah," muttered Wilkes. "Matter of fact. . . ."

He paused and rubbed the tips of his fin-

169

gers through his beard. His eyes were wistful.

"What happened to the bay mare?" asked Geraldi.

"Well, they drove her off, I guess," said Wilkes.

"Who drove her off?" asked Geraldi.

"Well, sir, there's some folks a bit rough around here in the mountains."

"Horse thieves, you mean?" questioned Geraldi.

"That's a mighty mean word to use. I dunno that I'd call 'em horse thieves."

"What did you have here in the way of livestock?"

"Why, I had three hosses, and there was a parcel of twenty-thirty sheep, and some goats, but I got rid of the pigs last year. They was always kind of smelly, like. Then there's always been a couple of cows. Old Mary Ann is all that I have left."

He pointed toward the door as though to indicate the cow that was browsing out of sight.

"What became of all that stock? Run off by the rough fellows of the mountains, eh?"

"I reckon so," Wilkes responded. His eyes avoided those of Geraldi as though in guilt.

"And they tried to burn you out, too, eh?"

"Yes, it looks that way," said Wilkes.

"How long ago?"

"About ten days."

"One minute," Geraldi said. He stared hard at the overalls that encased the helpless left leg of Wilkes. "Your son went off and left you, though he knew you were too crippled to move?" he asked in a soft, enticing voice.

"No, no. Sammy's kind of wild and careless, but he's a good fellow. My legs was both all right when he left."

Geraldi suddenly strode close.

"What's that hole that's punched through the leg of those overalls?" he demanded.

"That? Why, I dunno," said Wilkes. He moved a little back from Geraldi. On his face there was a more hunted look than before.

"You don't know? You do know!" cried Geraldi, and his voice rang suddenly and terribly through the cabin. "The same mountain fellows who ran off your cattle, put a bullet through you, and set fire to the barn, and left you here to burn!" He pointed a forefinger at Wilkes. "Answer me!" he thundered.

"Why . . . why," stammered Wilkes, "I reckon that's so. Only. . . ."

"And for ten days you have been starving and dying, inch by inch!" shouted Geraldi.

He picked up Wilkes in his arms, despite the feeble protests of the old man; the body was terribly light. On the nearer bunk he laid his burden, rolled up the overalls leg, and bared the wound. It was clumsily, but securely bandaged.

Something made Geraldi take off his hat; he dropped on one knee beside Wilkes and took the cold, bony hand of the old fellow in his.

Few people in this world had ever seen Geraldi tremble, but he was shaking now with a frightful passion.

"Stop worrying," entreated Geraldi. "I'm going to look up some of these rough fellows in the mountains, too. I'm going to gallop over the hill to Turnersville, and I'll be back inside of an hour and a half. I want to ask you two questions. Why didn't you butcher the cow for food?"

"Me . . . butcher Mary Ann?" said Wilkes. His old eyes opened wide. "Why, I wouldn't ever have thought of that. Mary Ann, she's been with me nigh onto sixteen years. No, seventeen. It was five years back that she had her last calf."

Geraldi took a long breath.

"And your son . . . your Sammy who goes off and leaves you alone . . . you say that he's never coming back?"

"Why, he'd come glad and willing," said Wilkes. "But I reckon that he won't be able."

"Why not?"

"Because he's going to die at sunset to-night, my poor Sammy," said Wilkes.

"Hold on . . . you mean that he's in prison . . . in a death house?"

"No, no. But it amounts to about the same. The trouble is a gent by name of Thurber. You ever hear of him?"

"Joe Thurber, the gunman? I've heard of him. I know all about him."

"Well, sir, when these gents up here in the mountains first started in trying to get us moved out of this here cabin, there was a ruction down in Turnersville one day, and my Sammy shot a fellow through the shoulder. That fellow was a friend of Joe Thurber. And Joe Thurber, he sends word that in a month from that day, he's going to meet up with Sammy in the main street of the town of El Gato, down in the desert by the border. And he's going to fill Sammy full of lead. He makes it a kind of a challenge. And I reckon that most of the Wilkes family don't like to take water from nobody. So Sammy, he went off to live for a month with his guns, and try to learn how to shoot faster and straighter, but he knew, and I know, that he'll never be able to beat Joe Thurber, that's killed so many men already."

"It's getting deeper and deeper, thicker and thicker," Geraldi commented. "But I want to know . . . why do these fellows in the mountains want to move you out of this place?"

"Partner," said Wilkes, "I dunno. I got no idea in the whole world, to tell you the truth."

Geraldi sprang to his feet and went to the door.

"I'm going to El Gato before sunset tonight," he promised. "And I'll keep Joe Thurber away from Sammy if I can. I'll stop at Turnersville on the way and send some stuff up to you. Lie still there, and don't you dare lift a hand. *¡Adiós!*"

He got to the roan gelding in a flash and, turning its head up the slope, galloped it mercilessly over the brow of the hill and then down the slant way to Turnersville.

Turnersville was just six shacks and a lean-to, but it had a general merchandise store. Geraldi looked at the round, brown face and the gray head of the man behind the counter and spoke to the point.

"Old man Wilkes has been hurt. I want a

good man sent up to him for a few days. Can you find the man for me inside of ten minutes?"

"Hank!" called the storekeeper.

A gangling fellow came through a rear door. His eyes were as blue as a mountain lake, and his cheeks were red. God kept his honest face smiling.

"There's the man," said the storekeeper.

"He suits me," Geraldi said. He took Hank by the hand, and into that hand emptied the contents of his wallet. It was a considerable sheaf of notes.

"Buy a horse," ordered Geraldi, "and load it with bacon, ham, potatoes, tinned stuff, crackers, flour, everything that you yourself would like to eat. Take your rifle and ammunition . . . you can shoot some fresh meat with it. Go up to the shack of Wilkes. You'll find him with a bullet hole in his leg. Take care of him as if he were your brother. You understand?"

"There's enough money here for a couple of years . . . ," began Hank.

"Spend what you want," said Geraldi, "and take ten dollars for every day you're on the job. They've tried to murder Wilkes and burn him out. If you can work up any information about that, I'll be glad to hear it and pay for it, when I come back here. So long. I'm in a hurry."

"Wait a minute. I don't even know your name!" cried Hank.

"It's better to have a man's money than to have his name," Geraldi called back as he fled through the door to the roan, which he mounted and rode rapidly away.

# II

## "EL GATO"

When Geraldi rode down through the foot-hills, he still felt that he had the matter well in hand, or would have by sunset. That was the moment when Sammy Wilkes and Joe Thurber had engaged to meet one another in the main street of the town of El Gato, and work with guns, knives, clubs, or bare hands until one or both of them were dead. And if Geraldi, by guile or by force, could prevent that meeting, he had determined to do so.

He was still a long distance from El Gato, but the roan mustang he rode was as fresh as the morning. Roans are a tough lot, and this one would not play out until it had pounded through many miles of desert dust and fire. Through a gap in the hills as through a gun sight, Geraldi could see the white blaze of the desert commencing, and he was just hardening his mind to it when the roan stepped into a hole and pitched forward on its head.

There was a hundredth part of a second

for Geraldi to act. In that time he freed his feet from the stirrups; and on those feet and his hands he landed like a cat. The roan was trying to get up, but continually falling over to the right. With flaring nostrils and with burning eyes, it strove to rise and failed, and would always fail, for its right leg was broken below the knee.

A revolver slid into Geraldi's hand. He took one look at the patch of pale fire that appeared beyond the hills, and then he faced the horse. Twice he raised the muzzle of the gun; twice it sank down again. He had to walk to the side of the roan, and, as it continued to struggle, he shot it accurately through the temple.

After that, he sat on a rock and smoked a cigarette half through. He was summoning his resolution, fixing his mind, tempering his will to steel.

Then he stamped on the fuming butt and set to work. He pulled the saddle and bridle from the dead body, climbed a rock heap, and cached them in a deep crevice. He stripped himself naked and showed a body as brown and stringy and lean as a desert Indian's. From a saddlebag he took out a loincloth and a pair of good moccasins. These he put on. And now, except for the blue of his eyes and the shortness of his black hair, he looked like an Indian, indeed.

He hesitated over two things. One was a canteen that he could sling over his shoulder. But he knew where several water holes were, or ought to be, and a canteen thumping against his body for so many miles would be a torment. He lingered another moment over the gun. When he got to El Gato, he had to have some sort of a tool to work with; besides, he loved that gun. He knew it like a brother. It shot a little high and to the right, but he could always make allowances for that fault. Guns, like women, are never perfect. However, he discarded the gun, also. Last of all, he opened his wallet, but already he knew that it was empty.

So at length he started down through the last foothills wearing only the moccasins and the loincloth. Within the folds of that loincloth, however, he concealed certain slivers of the finest steel, without which Geraldi was never known to operate. The day that had seemed comfortably full of hours was now terribly abbreviated, but he did not run a step until he came out into the glare of the desert. The sun made a high light on each shoulder. It scorched him like a burning glass. It cooked his left side and would continue to broil him there until noon, when it would take the other flank. He knew all of these things when he commenced to run.

He jogged a hundred yards, walked a furlong, jogged a furlong, walked a hundred yards, then stepped out with a frictionless, reaching stride that he never could have learned from a white man. Once in that gait, it seemed impossible for him to vary it.

His nostrils widened as his wind left him. His body pinched a little to the left as a pain began to stab him between the ribs. But he clung to the same pace for ten miles, at the end of which he found a water hole with green scum blanketing it. He lay flat and pawed a trench in the soft sand close to the edge of the pool. In a few minutes, clear water seeped into it. The taste of it was bad even after this filtering, but it was life to the runner.

When he stood up, a moment's dizziness made the horizon mountains spin, and he half wondered if he had been well advised in leaving his hat behind him. But his head cleared at once. He saw behind him the hills he had left already turning from brown to blue, and miles away the heads of the Devil Mountains were little purple spikes above the line of earth and sky. The first ten miles had left a slight tremor in his body.

He continued with the same changeless stride. A desert jack rabbit, made of bone, sinew, and brown fluff, started out from a clump of mesquite and showed him the way to split the breeze toward El Gato.

White men lean forward when they run, and this leaning kills them with their own weight. The Indian is erect above the hips. He breathes with less effort, and he keeps in easier balance. Geraldi ran like an Indian.

It was a long way to more water. He began to feel the gaunt hollows in his cheeks before he reached it. Now he sat in the midst of that immeasurable plain with the range he had left and the Devil Mountains an equal height in the sky and an equal blue. He got up and ran again.

He was deep in his second wind. He squinted his eyes hard to keep out the sun's glare, beating up from the sand. Then he passed through a sweep of blue-gray greasewood, like smoke on the face of the ground.

The miles went behind him, slowly. The mountains stood still, before him and behind. He was on a treadmill, consuming power but covering no ground. He told himself that he would not look at the Devil Mountains for two hours.

He kept that promise to himself, looking

forward hungrily to that great moment as to the unveiling of a treasure. All those hours he ran without faltering, without slowing, without changing his stride. He began to grin with the agony of the effort, but he persisted, as one who had tested himself many a time before, and knew how much the steel of his being could be wrenched and bent before it broke.

He reached one of those rare gifts from God to the desert, a natural spring that bubbled up and ran a hundred yards before the sands drank the last of it with dry, crinkling lips. There he drank. He bathed himself, watched the shuddering of his body come to an end, and ran on again. It was the middle of the afternoon. The sands and rocks that had drunk up the sun all day now burned the feet of Geraldi through the thin soles of the moccasins, but could not keep those feet from flying on toward El Gato.

The Devil Mountains had turned from blue to brown, and the shadows in the gorges were to his eye like cold water to his throat. He had run by sheer strength of his will. Now he began to run for victory, like the marathon runner who sees hope in the last mile, after he has despaired for ten.

He reached the pass that cleaves the Devil Mountains with an axe stroke. Shadows sloped over him now, like a blessing, and at the mouth of the gorge a wind struck his face. He saw the blue line of the creek, he saw the white houses and green trees of El Gato, he saw the yellow river and naked, sunburned Mexico beyond.

He was ahead, he was far ahead of his time. The sun was westering, but it was high above the horizon. Yet he kept to the same long-striding gait that had carried him over the desert. When he reached the creek, he waded in to his hips, rinsed out his throat, and swallowed a few gulps — not enough to slake his thirst but to take the agony of it away.

Then he climbed out on the farther bank, nearer the town, and stretched his legs in the heat of the sun, his body in the shadow of a tree.

His hands were empty of weapons. His body was almost naked. But before sunset, he had to enter the town and stop two gunmen. No mere gesture would make them halt. There was murder in their hearts.

He refused to think of that problem, however. For one hour he contemplated nothing but the green heaven of the tree above him, letting his glance wander contentedly among the branches as over a promised land. When he sat up, the tremor was gone from him. He kneeled by the creek and drank deeply. His lungs were cool. Breathing was a delight. But yonder in the west the sun was turning to gold. Time was short for Geraldi.

To be seen in this garb was to make himself a spectacle, and public attention was what he must avoid. So he scouted along the bank of the creek until he found what he wanted — laundry set out on the bushes by Mexican women to dry.

He took a pair of white cotton trousers and a ragged shirt. For that garb, bare feet would be more appropriate than moccasins, so he thrust his footgear into a bush, rolled up the sleeves of his shirt to the elbow, and pulled his black hair over his forehead. When he walked into El Gato, he looked like a handsome Mexican youth of twenty-five, or less.

Excitement took the place of sleep and food, to rest and nourish him. His first task now was to equip himself with a gun.

That should be no great task, for one with Geraldi's peculiar endowments and training. When he got into the main street of the town, in fact, he found that it was already crowded with armed men who formed groups, which dissolved and reformed. The sun was reddening in the west now, and the moment was not far distant. The spectators had gathered, and the two main actors would not be long off the stage. In this shifting crowd, every man had a revolver, either a lump inside his clothes, or a big Colt holstered in full view on his right thigh. Geraldi made selection of one of the latter in the midst of a close pack of men. It meant the unbuttoning of the top flap of the holster, and the gentle easing of the gun out of its leather case, but this Geraldi had accomplished with two gestures of the supple fingers of his left hand. The gun itself slid into the looseness of his over-size shirt, and he went on.

A sudden uproar started behind him. Someone began to shout that he had been robbed. People gathered, and, as they packed in close, Geraldi sifted through the little mob attracted by the jingling of coins in unguarded pockets, here and there. He helped himself with the same ghostly ease. When he found gold, he returned it. When he found silver, he took it and counted it with the tips of his sensitive fingers as it accumulated. When the sum rose to six dollars, he left that crowd and went his way.

At a tobacco shop he bought a sack of tobacco, a package of brown straw papers, a little cube of sulphur matches from California, and two bars of chocolate that he ate greedily. He was masticating the last of them and lighting a cigarette when he drifted into a patch of white-shirted Mexican laborers on a street corner. They were all talking rapidly, but in murmurs, for one could never tell what white men would do if they made too much noise.

"Which way does Thurber come?" Geraldi asked of a round-faced brown man.

The Mexican looked at the ragged shirt and then at the blue eyes of Geraldi. It had been in perfect Spanish that Geraldi asked the question, but the blue eyes were too much for the other. He turned his back abruptly. It was a white-headed old *peón* who muttered: "The river road, my son. The river road."

In a moment, Geraldi was out of the Mexican group and swinging away for the river road. As he went, he heard distant roars of excitement, and knew that Sammy Wilkes must have reached one end of the town.

There was not very much to El Gato. In a few moments Geraldi was clear of it and pacing in his bare feet down the river road through dust that had not yet had a chance to lose the heat of the day.

Cottonwoods grew at one side of the road

with high shrubbery between the trunks, and, looking westward through the brush, Jimmy Geraldi saw the sun drop to the horizon as a great red ball, with its crimson cheeks distorted. That sense of a red fire was with him, at his right hand, when he saw a dust cloud, down the winding road, dissolve and a galloping horseman appear from it.

Geraldi stood in the middle of the road and waved both arms frantically.

# III

## "ON THE RIVER ROAD"

Joe Thurber was a big, determined man, and he rode on a big, determined horse that shook the ground with the beat of its hoofs. But Thurber brought the horse to a stop in a swirl of dust that powdered the clothes of Geraldi with white. There was a workman-like look about Thurber in his shirt of faded-blue flannel, his bandanna, his unshaven, dark face with the scowl between his brows that comes of striving to shade one's eyes against the desert sun. He wore a pair of leather chaps, scarred with thorn scratches, and only his boots and spurs were beautiful, as fine as money could buy. On the reins, his left hand was gloved, but his right hand was bare in case the revolver that was on his thigh should be needed suddenly.

"What's up?" he barked.

Geraldi smiled. "I have news for you, Joe."

The big Colt that he had stolen flashed in his hand as he spoke. Thurber's own hand dropped to the butt of his holstered gun, but it remained there, hesitant, while the free hand of Geraldi passed across his forehead, wiping away the black hair that had been falling over it.

"Geraldi!" Joe Thurber exclaimed suddenly, and lifted both hands above his head. Staring bitterly down at the face of Geraldi, he continued: "Wilkes turned yellow, eh? Sammy hired you to do his killing for him. Is that it?"

"Wilkes never heard of me," said Geraldi. "Unbuckle that gun belt, Joe, and let it drop."

"Everybody has heard of you, Jimmy," said Thurber. "The day's gone by when you could drift around and not be known, sooner or later. You've raised too much hell."

He complied with the order, slowly unbuckling the gun belt and allowing it to drop to the dust. And he groaned when he was disarmed, saying: "He's waiting for me in there. He's putting up a show of waiting, I mean to say. But the hound knows that he wouldn't dare to stop for me, except that you're out here doing his dirty work. Even Chinamen will stand up to me, after this evening. I'll have the name of a yellow dog, if I don't show up. Geraldi, give me a

189

chance. Sammy Wilkes is sashaying up and down the main street, by this time, and telling the world that I'm a coward, and the world will have to believe what he says."

"Wilkes didn't hire me," Geraldi said. "Wilkes doesn't know that I have anything to do with this job. Dismount and move your hands carefully, Joe. And do everything slowly, as if you wanted pictures taken."

As he spoke, he made small gestures with the Colt that he was holding at half arm's length before him. But although the weapon was not sighted at Thurber, merely pointed, he regarded it with a frozen awe, and dismounted exactly as he had been commanded. His big black stallion tossed its crest and stamped, raising a double cloud of dust.

"What's the deal to be?" Thurber asked uneasily.

"Back up," ordered Geraldi.

Thurber backed up several paces. Stooping swiftly, Geraldi picked up the fallen holster and threw it into the dust at Thurber's feet. He let his own Colt now fall from his hand and added: "There you are, Joe. That's an even break. You've got your gun before you, and mine is in the same place. You've killed nine men, and here's your chance for an extra number."

Thurber's arms and shoulders twitched. He seemed about to stoop for the gun, but slowly straightened himself again. His swarthy face had turned a yellow-green.

"Nobody has an even start with you, Geraldi," he said at last. "You're better than the rest of us, and you know it."

"You've been a lot better than most of the fellows you've bumped off," said Geraldi. "It's never been a fair fight. It wouldn't have been a fair fight tonight, between you and Wilkes."

"He's gone out and killed his men," argued Thurber.

"He has plenty of fighting nerve," Geraldi answered, "but he hasn't spent three hours a day for ten years handling a revolver, and you know that's what you've done. Wilkes has done some honest work."

Thurber licked his lips and cleared his throat.

"Well, what's next?" he asked.

"You won't fight?"

"No. I'm damned if I fight. You've got me dead the second you go for your gun, and I know it. There's nobody around here to see me quitting . . . and I quit!"

"I won't call you names," Geraldi said slowly.

"It wouldn't do any good," answered Thurber. "I won't fight. Not unless there's somebody around to report on what I'm doing."

Geraldi fitted a toe under his fallen gun, kicked it in the air, and caught it in his hand.

Thurber grunted, and blinked at the flicker of red sunset light on the gun. "I know about your tricks, Geraldi," he said. "You've got plenty of tricks, and you've left plenty of dead men behind you. It ain't a fight when you meet another man. It's just a murder."

Geraldi caused the heavy gun to disappear inside the loose shirt that he was wearing. He stepped up to Thurber, and deliberately and rapidly fanned him, and, while he searched Thurber, every instant his insolent blue eyes were defying the gunman to resist.

It was a vast temptation for Thurber. He was a powerful fellow, with some forty pounds more substance than the hundred and sixty or seventy pounds that made up Geraldi. But he knew something about what those slender, flashing hands could do, and he very wisely resisted temptation. So Geraldi stepped back with a small cargo of loot.

It consisted of a new bandanna, clean and

folded, a good sheath knife, razor-sharp, a bit of oiled silk containing matches, and a considerable wealth in greenbacks. With the tip of a finger, Geraldi flicked the corners of the bills up and read the denominations with an uncanny speed.

"What's been the lucky play lately, Thurber?" he asked. "How many Mexican throats did you have to cut to collect eleven hundred and forty bucks?"

Thurber looked bitterly from the money to the face of the man who had taken it. The wrong word came to his throat, and he blurted it out.

"You damn' thief!" he snarled.

Geraldi shook his head. "I'm not a thief. I'm a frigate bird," he said, smiling.

"You're a what?" growled Thurber.

"I live on the other thieves, not on the honest men, Joe. That's what the frigate bird does. It hangs high in the air, and, when the fish hawk has a good, fat fish in its hooks, the frigate bird swoops off its perch in the sky and scares the hawk into dropping the loot. Then the frigate bird snatches it out of the air as it drops. And that's my business, Joe. You never made an honest dollar in your life, so I'll make free with some of your crooked money."

"When some of us get you, one of these

days," said Thurber, "we're going to get you good."

"I know that," agreed Geraldi. "I know that someday the crooks will get me and eat me raw. But till they do, I lead a happy life, old son."

"How many men want to get you, Geraldi?" asked Thurber, his curiosity almost equal to his rage.

"About a dozen of your caliber, Joe," Geraldi responded. "And there are half a dozen of a higher cut, and three of the so-called master minds. As for the general run of yeggs, pickpockets, safe crackers, tramps, hold-up artists, second-story men, black-mailers, counterfeiters, fellows who shove the queer, confidence men, and the rest . . . why, I don't know. I suppose the number of 'em goes into hundreds . . . fellows whose fish I've caught after they've done the fishing."

"You call yourself honest, I guess? A regular upholder of the law, eh? Why, you ain't anything more than a fence!" cried Joe Thurber. "You take the stolen goods, that's all."

"I give back a lot of it to the people who've been robbed," answered Geraldi. "But a lot of times I don't know who's lost the hard cash. Here's one instance, you see. I don't know what pockets you've dipped into in old Mexico, Joe, so the whole chunk of money is mine. I don't have to feel any prickings of conscience."

He picked up Thurber's fallen gun, and mounted the black horse.

"A horse thief, too, are you?" said Thurber. For it was a good horse, and this last loss was almost more than Thurber could bear.

"So long, Joe!" Geraldi called. "I've an idea that we'll be meeting again, though I don't suppose you'll be showing your handsome face in El Gato for a while. People won't be glad to see you there, Joe. They'll be apt to point their fingers at you. As for me, if I catch you on the trail of young Sammy Wilkes ever again, I'll shoot you on sight. *¡Adiós!*"

# IV

## "THE CELEBRATION"

Geraldi had no desire to take the black horse in along the river road, so he cut across country, and came in by a winding trail until he found a livery stable that backed against the creek.

"My *señor* wants to leave this horse here," he said. "He wants you to feed it oats, not crushed barley."

"Who's your *señor*, kid?" asked one of the loungers at the wide, lantern-lighted doorway.

"*Señor* Garavan," Geraldi responded, and disappeared.

He came to the surface of the life of El Gato again, in quite another part of the town, and that was the main street, which was attracting a lot of attention and making a lot of noise, this evening.

For young Sammy Wilkes with his red head and his freckled face and his big, capable shoulders had been seen to ride up and down that main street from end to end, all through the red of the sunset, and until the full dark of the night descended, bringing down the stars, and no one had stood out to encounter him during that brave vigil. No Joe Thurber had appeared.

All the scores of men who had traveled that day from a distance, so that they might witness history made by guns and written in smoke and blood, could not allow the occasion to pass unnoticed, and, therefore, they gave Wilkes a party. They threw the party, and they threw it big. It was a day that might have written the name of El Gato into the permanent annals of the region. As it was, El Gato decided that it would stage as large an explosion as possible, in a fairly peaceful way. And the town succeeded in making a great noise.

Geraldi, arriving on the outskirts of a gaudy scene, found that Sammy was already well beyond the mood in which he could listen to reason.

For when Geraldi worked close to him, and said: "I've got something to tell you. Your father is. . . ."

"Old men and business tomorrow!" Sammy interrupted with a shout, and sent Geraldi spinning away from him.

"Old men and business tomorrow!" echoed another hearty voice, and the speaker with a powerful swing of his foot kicked Geraldi straight through the swinging doors.

He landed fairly in the face of an entering squad who tried to kick him back through the doors once more, they were so enraged to have a Mexican flung in their faces, as it were. But Geraldi slithered away from the hands and feet that reached for him.

In the darkness of the next street corner he leaned against a wall, panting, and recalled with considerable vividness the face of the man who had kicked him. He was a big man, with a red face and a swollen red neck that bulged out beneath his ears. He had the mouth of a catfish and the eyes of a hungry pig.

Geraldi swore very softly to himself, and carved the picture of that man in his mind.

The party issued noisily from the saloon in a procession. Sammy Wilkes was being borne aloft on the shoulders of his friends, but no farther did the procession wind than to the next saloon. When it entered that place, Geraldi glided in at the tail of the crowd. He made himself as invisible as possible in corners, and saw the party turn to gambling.

Sammy Wilkes had spent everything except his last ten dollars. He went to the roulette wheel in the back room of the saloon, and turned that ten dollars into three hundred and fifty by playing the "seven." That good luck encouraged him to play odd and even, and he swelled the three hundred and fifty into twenty-eight hundred in the course of five minutes, when he returned to the bar to buy drinks for everyone, for the entire town.

But the town would not have his drinks. The order of the day was that his money was no good in El Gato. Everything that he wanted was free. The house set up the liquor, or some ready wallet was always at hand to pay.

But twenty-eight hundred dollars was too much money to lie easily in the pockets of any man, and Geraldi noticed that certain faces in the crowd looked at Sammy Wilkes with an envious eye. There was, above all, the fellow of the bulging neck and the mouth of a catfish.

He attached himself closely to Wilkes. He was to be seen resting a hand upon Sammy's shoulder, nudging him in the ribs, entering into the enjoyment with the loudest laughter of the evening. Moreover, his glance wandered covertly but affectionately, now and then, to the well-filled pockets of Sammy Wilkes.

Geraldi from his shadowy corners noted

all this with an eye a little sharper than that of a hawk.

Then, suddenly, trouble loomed before him. It came in the shape of a sandy-haired man with a very short nose and an immensely long jaw, a man who, when he spoke, used only one side of his mouth.

He appeared before Geraldi and shook a finger at him.

"Hey, Al! Hey, Blondy!" he shouted. "Come and look here!"

Blondy had the pale, thin hands of a gambler and a ministerial solemnity of face and manner.

"What's the matter, Stew?" he asked.

"Look at him!" exclaimed Stew. "I wanna know . . . suppose he was slicked up in good clothes, wouldn't that stand as a ringer for Slim Jim?"

"You mean for Jim Geraldi?" demanded Blondy.

"That's what I mean!" cried Stew.

He backed up a little as he spoke. One might have thought, from the manner of Stew, that Geraldi was a package of dynamite with a burning fuse hitched to it. Blondy, also, was much shocked by the very name that he had just pronounced. He also recoiled, shrinking close to Stew in the manner of one who needed help for a desperate last stand.

"No, Jim Geraldi's bigger," said Blondy. "He's taller, and he's much heavier."

"You've seen him in action," protested Stew, "and then he always looks bigger than human . . . but, by thunder, that's Geraldi to the tips of his fingers!"

"What have I done, *señor?*" asked Jimmy Geraldi. "I am only a poor Mexican. I mean no harm, and I stood near to watch the happy noise and to smell the whisky. What have I done?"

He began to cringe away along the wall, when another man took notice — he of the catfish mouth, who came up, exclaiming: "Who named Geraldi?"

"I did, Pooch," said Stew. "This fellow here is a ringer for him. I've seen that devil, Geraldi, and I've seen him work, too."

"If I thought that was Geraldi," said Pooch, "I'd break him in two. I've got reasons for doing it. He's the one that killed Rufe Thomas in Tombstone. But this feller ain't Geraldi. I've kicked him out of one saloon, and I'm going to kick him out of another one."

He strode forward. His eyes were more like the savage glare of a swine than ever before. He came with his big red fist poised to deliver a blow, and Geraldi shrank before him, putting both arms before his face, lifting one knee as if to guard against a kick to the body. Some of the half-drunken men laughed loudly. Some sneered. But young Sammy Wilkes shouted above the uproar: "Don't you hit him, Pooch! Leave him alone! He's only a poor Mex!"

This only made Pooch rush in with more determination, and he struck with all his might. It seemed as though his fist went straight through the head of Geraldi, who had winced a little to the side at the last moment. At any rate, Pooch smote the wall with a blow that made it shudder and brought a screech of pain from him.

Geraldi, shrinking away, was caught by the mischievous hands of other men, and held for the avenger.

"The sneak, I'm going to kill him!" screamed Pooch. "I'm going to tear him in two! Leave me at him and. . . ."

He struck with his uninjured fist, this time, and aimed the blow well at Geraldi's jaw. It went home solidly, in all seeming. At least there was no eye so professionally fast that it was able to notice how, at the last minute, Geraldi's head jerked to the side, riding with the punch. And, turned in this fashion from a blow to a push, Geraldi was hurled to the floor.

Big Pooch leaped after him. Pooch was wearing heavy boots with formidable spurs, and he knew exactly how to use toe, heel, and spur in trembling and cutting up a fighter who struck the floor. But Geraldi had struck the floor rolling, and he got up beyond the tangle of the crowd, slipping out through the swinging doors with a wild cry for help and for mercy.

In the outer darkness, Geraldi skidded through an alley, swung himself over a back yard fence, and rounded toward the rear of the saloon from which he had just been thrown. He could not return publicly, now, to that crowd. He would be too marked. His presence a third time among the celebrants would be an impertinence to be punished with mob violence.

He was quivering through every part of his body. As he went past a window, the dull glow from the inside showed his brown face cruelly set.

Through a barroom window, he saw Pooch nursing an injured left hand, still cursing and shaking his head over it. He saw the men laughing, saw the red-brown flash of the whisky rising to their lips, saw the colorful gleaming of the bottles behind the bar and in the mirror that reflected them. And all the while that savage hunger was increasing in him, making him breathe hard and fast. He had come there to watch over Sammy Wilkes and the dangerous cargo of wealth that Sammy had picked up; he found himself staying less for that reason than for another.

But big Sammy Wilkes had grown suddenly half sober. He stood gloomily at the bar for a moment, then slipped away, and went through the front door almost unnoticed.

He was not entirely unregarded, however. All the others seemed preoccupied, but Pooch was too interested in his quarry to have his attention distracted even by an injured hand. Instantly he was out of the swinging doors in pursuit.

Geraldi followed. He saw Wilkes striding with long, unbalanced steps along the street. Behind Wilkes a shadow lurked from doorway to doorway. Upon the heels of that shadow Geraldi was presently moving with a footfall as soundless as the padded step of a cat. At the entrance to a blind alley he leaped and struck with the barrel of his revolver. Pooch fell in a sodden heap. Geraldi, lifting that ponderous, loose bulk in his arms, carried it a few paces deeper into the darkness and dropped it to the ground. Then he returned to the trail of Sammy Wilkes.

# V

# "A KILLER'S LUCK"

Under the sign of the hotel, Wilkes disappeared. Geraldi, sitting on his heels across the street, waited until a certain window of the façade was lighted. Then he crossed the street whose dust flowed over his naked feet like cool, ghostly water.

It was a hard climb up the face of the hotel. But toes helped him as much as fingers, taking advantage of every small purchase, until he was outside the open, lighted window. He saw the shadow of Wilkes waver across the room, and peered cautiously inside.

There was distinctly too much liquor in Sammy Wilkes. His burly, rather handsome face was flushed with it, his mouth was loose, his eyes were unfocused. His knees sagging, his body swaying, he leaned above the lamp, and blew it out. Through the darkness, Geraldi heard him recross the room, heard him crack against a chair, heard him tumble his weight on the bed.

The springs creaked loudly a few times. Then followed silence, and through that silence the sound of regularly drawn, hard breathing.

Geraldi slid through the window. He had mapped the room in his mind, so that he knew the distances from the window to the bed and to the washstand, the bit of worn matting on which the table stood, the position of the two chairs — until one of them had been knocked out of place by Wilkes.

In the darkness of the room, he did not strain his eyes, but closed them and moved like the truly blind by the sense of touch alone. It was better to do that in the beginning, and get the last glare of light out of the optic centers before he tried seeing in the dark.

He found the displaced chair, registered its new location with caution and care, and then got to the farthest corner of the room and stretched himself on the floor.

Men can fix an hour for awakening, and, when it comes, their power of will rattles an alarm in the brain. Now Geraldi fixed his attention half on the window, half toward the door. Having done that, he made his body relax. He began with his breathing, which he made smooth, even, free. By the calm touch of his will, he made his heart steadier in beat and stronger. He loosened the hardened muscles of stomach and back. He let his shoulders spill as loosely as sand. He took the strain out of the tendons in his neck, undid the tremors in his arms, caused his legs to stretch in utter relaxation.

The moment he had accomplished this, he fell soundly asleep, except for that inner guardian of the unconscious that he had posted to keep watch over his slumber. But his sleep was not like that of a nervous beast of prey, fitful, causing him to waken with starts. Instead, his repose was absolute. That skill in relaxation had taught him how to condense into one hour the repose that most people cannot win from two or three.

What wakened him was a very small scratching sound. It brought his eyes wide open, every sense alert, and his brain cleared of fatigue by even this short sleep.

The noise came from the door. It was very soft, but repeated. Presently, as he rose to his feet, he heard a louder noise, and knew that the bolt had been deliberately slid, inside the lock.

The bare feet of Geraldi carried him noiselessly to the side of the door. The knob of it was turning. He could see by a dull shaft of light that came from across the street and painted a faintly glimmering highlight on the brass of the doorknob. It turned, and the door sagged open inch by inch. Sammy Wilkes was snoring softly, as though sleep were a husky fountain, rising, ebbing, regurgitating.

"It's all right. He's sleeping like a pig," someone whispered in the hall. "I'll do the job. Go down and get the hosses."

"Don't take no chances," another voice replied. "Bash his head in for him. Then you'll make sure of getting the dough. Better let me come in and. . . ."

"G'wan and get the hosses. Going to teach me my business?"

A bulk of shadow crept through the doorway; the door was closed behind it. From the hall, Geraldi could feel, rather than hear, the weight of departing footfalls. He made himself smaller as the big intruder separated himself from the greater darkness of the wall, and stepped out into the interior of the room.

The left hand of the man was empty. Geraldi could see this clearly. In the right hand was the revolver with which the skull of Wilkes was to be smashed. It was gripped by the barrel.

Now the shadowy outline grew suddenly smaller. The man had crouched, taking instinctively a beast-like attitude as he moved forward toward his beastly work. Geraldi advanced behind him with no weapon. He had used the weight of a gun barrel on the head of Pooch, not because he needed such a tool when he took a man by surprise, but because he had a grudge against that brute of a man. Now, with the edge of his palm, he struck the wrist of this killer. He struck it hard, straight across the spring of the tendon. With his other hand he caught the revolver as it slid out of fingers whose strength was suddenly stolen.

That shadowy bulk whirled with a hiss of indrawn breath. Geraldi struck again with the edge of the palm of his right hand. The light was obscure; the target was hard to find, but by a sort of instinct he knew that he would reach the mark. Just behind the base of the jaw, and just beneath the ear, where the neck swells out to its widest, there is a point where vital nerves spring up close to the surface of the flesh, and it was exactly across this point that Geraldi's hand whipped like the stroke of an iron-bound ruler.

The intruder slumped heavily to his knees, flinging his arms around Geraldi's legs. Geraldi leaned, chose his target with deliberation, and struck again, this time at the back of the neck, as the head of his victim bowed over. Then he stepped back and allowed the loose bulk of the man to settle down upon the floor.

There was a sudden creaking sound on the bed. The snoring ceased.

A quick, frightened voice called out: "What the devil's there?"

"A friend," Geraldi answered, "and a gunman who's stumbled over some bad luck. Hurry up and light the lamp."

Heavy feet thumped on the floor. A match scratched on a trouser leg, leaving a vanishing streak of phosphorus. The flame spurted blue, flared out with yellow, the lamp was lighted and filled the room with brilliance.

It showed Geraldi on his knees beside the bulk that lay face down. Sammy Wilkes had a gun in a tremulous hand. His eyes were sober, his face pinched with the shock of fear.

"Got a bit of twine?" asked Geraldi.

"Yes. Who are you?"

"I'm the fellow that was kicked out of one saloon and thrown out of another."

"You're no Mex. What . . . ?"

Wilkes pulled from a pocket a wad of bills, reached deeper, and produced a length of strong twine.

"Who's that?" he gasped.

"We're going to find out," Geraldi answered.

With the twine he lashed the wrists of the fallen man across the small of his back. The victim regained consciousness with a low moan in his throat. Geraldi turned him on his back, took another revolver from a spring holster under the pit of the right arm, and then ordered him to rise.

The man struggled to his feet and stood uncertainly, breathing with difficulty, muttering incoherently. He was the color of a half-breed, but his eyes were those of a white man. A nameless grossness and brutality filled his handsome face, and a shag of his long black hair drooped over his shoulder.

"When you picked up twenty-eight hundred dollars last night," said Geraldi, "I thought I'd follow you, Wilkes. That fellow Pooch was the first man at your heels. I rapped him over the head and left him in an alley to cool off. Then I climbed up the front of the hotel, and slipped through the window while you were asleep. Presently the lock was picked, and this chap came in. I thought that it would be Pooch again, but I was wrong. Who are you, brother?"

The other heaved his shoulders, trying to get his hands free, so that gestures could help his conversation. "My name's Ray

Tucker," he said, staring at the bare, brown feet of Geraldi. "I'm from the Panhandle. Well, I was just down here and I saw Wilkes get a big wad of money, and I thought it would be a pretty good time to pick up a stake without working very hard or long for it. So I just come up here and picked the lock, the way the Mex says. And I come in. What did you slug me with?"

He glared at Geraldi as he spoke.

"With my hand," Geraldi said.

"You lie!" exclaimed Tucker.

Geraldi extended his lean hand and looked down at the muscle that projected along the edge of the palm.

"Here's a job for the sheriff to take a look at," suggested Sammy Wilkes. "If you'll hold him here while I go and get. . . ."

"Wait a minute," Geraldi interrupted. "Stand over here in the light, Tucker, I want to look at your pretty face."

"I'll stay where I am," said Tucker. "You can get the sheriff, and be damned to you."

Geraldi sat on the edge of the table and made a cigarette, all the while surveying the face of his captive.

"I'd better get the . . . ," Sammy Wilkes began.

"Be quiet," said Geraldi. He was not insolent. He was simply preserving the train of his thoughts from interruption.

"Ever in Mexico?" he asked Ray Tucker.

"Yeah. Maybe," said Tucker.

"Speak out and give me direct answers. You don't know the boots you're standing in."

"What boots?"

"It won't be robbery you'll be charged with. It'll be intent to murder."

"You can't charge that," said Tucker. "I only. . . ."

"I heard you talk to the fellow in the hall, the one that's getting the horses ready. Where are those horses, by the way?"

"I don't know."

"You better talk to me, partner," said Geraldi. "I don't want to be violent."

"I'll talk to you when I get in court," said Tucker.

"You can see how confident he is," Geraldi remarked to Sammy Wilkes. "That's because he knows that he has some mighty big people behind him."

Wilkes, utterly uncertain, bewildered, sober, stood by the lamp with eyes still rounded.

"I want to know exactly where the horses are," Geraldi said to the prisoner.

"I'm done answering questions," replied Tucker.

"All right," Geraldi said to Wilkes. "It doesn't matter. This fellow doesn't want to talk. I'll just put him out of pain, and then go down to get the other rat. When the man with the horses sees this one dead, he'll be apt to talk a little more freely, and conversation is the first thing that we want right now."

He drew Thurber's knife, as he spoke, and stepped straight to Tucker. That yellow face grew yellower still, and two streaks that had been almost imperceptible before now stood out white upon his cheek.

"Wait!" yipped Tucker.

"Where are the horses?" repeated Geraldi.

"By thunder, who are you?" breathed Tucker.

"A man with a knife. Answer up, you mangy rat!"

"The hosses are back behind the barn," said Tucker. "Alf would be bringing them from out of the trees, by this time. He'd. . . ."

"That's enough. I'll go down and bring back Alf," Geraldi said. "Watch this fellow, Wilkes. Watch him like a rattlesnake in hot weather, because he's full of poison. You'll find out that he's one of the gang who has been trying to make your father move off his place . . . the same gang that had Thurber send you the challenge. After you left the mountains, they raided the farm, shot your father, ran off the cattle, and put a match to the barn, to burn the body."

"You mean my father's dead?" Wilkes asked, his voice beginning loudly and dwindling to nothing on the last word.

"He's alive," Geraldi assured him. "But watch this snake, and don't you dare let him talk till I get back with Alf."

# VI

## "DEATH FROM THE DARK"

Geraldi went down the back stairs of the hotel and found the rear door locked, the key gone. He slid out a window instead, dropped ten feet to the ground, light as a cat, and struck off for the high, looming shadow of the barn. At the rear corner of it he waited, and saw, exactly as Ray Tucker had supposed, a big man issuing from the darkness of the woods on the other side of a pasture.

Geraldi waited for him to come closer. The night had turned hotter. A wind was rising. The stars were mere needlepoints that looked down through a mist of dust. But they gave enough light to show the stranger taking off his coat, then throwing it over the saddle of one of the two horses, for the night was very warm.

Geraldi drew a gun, then slid the weapon out of sight again. Noise was not what he wanted, but all the privacy that silence could give him. So he took out the knife that had belonged to Joe Thurber and held it on the flat of his hand after the fashion of Mexican knife throwers. Then he walked out toward the stranger, constantly keeping one of the horses between him and Alf's line of sight.

He was very close when a subdued voice asked: "That you, Ray?"

"Yes," Geraldi responded.

His voice or his difference in size caused Alf to exclaim: "The devil you are!" And like one who has only one resource when in doubt, Alf pulled a gun.

At the dull flash of it in the starlight, Geraldi flicked the knife in a gleaming line that went out at the right shoulder of Alf. The wounded man dropped his gun into his left hand, uttered a faint, whining sound, and leaped on the back of the nearer horse. In an instant he was fading into the night as fast as a hard gallop could snatch him away.

Geraldi gathered the reins of the second horse to follow, but changed his mind. He had other work to finish in the hotel at once. In the grass he found the knife that had slashed Alf's shoulder, and with this and the coat that had been left over the saddle of the second horse, he returned to the hotel. He climbed easily to the window by which he had departed, and so went back to the room of Sammy Wilkes.

He found the pair lost in a gloomy silence. Ray Tucker, rolling up his eyes at Geraldi, saw the latter cross the room, pick up a scrap of paper, and start to wipe a red stain of blood from the blade of his knife.

"You've killed him!" breathed Ray Tucker. "You've stabbed poor Alf!"

Geraldi said nothing. The face of Sammy Wilkes was gray and red in patches, and he looked the questions that did not reach his lips. But Geraldi, calmly going through Alf's coat that he had brought with him, laid on the central table half a plug of chewing tobacco, a stubby pencil, a little notebook from which many pages had been torn, a handkerchief, some matches and an old pipe, a wallet that held only a few greenbacks of small denomination, and a grimy envelope that contained a slip of paper on which was written in a cramped hand: **If you get him, show this to Silas Wisner and he'll understand.**

Geraldi read the thing aloud, and translated to Wilkes: "If they get you, Sammy, they're to take this paper to Silas Wisner, and he'll pay them off. Is that right, Tucker?"

Tucker chewed on his nether lip. He shrugged his shoulders and studied the face of Geraldi with a desperate interest.

"You don't have to confess," said Geraldi. "The money that you found on Wilkes would not have been your only reward. What was Wisner to have paid to you?"

Tucker cleared his throat. He stared at Geraldi more wildly than ever, exclaiming: "Say, partner! I wouldn't know about all of these here things!"

"Thurber, Tucker, Pooch, and the rest of 'em," said Geraldi, "are not doing this work for themselves. They've got somebody behind them with brains. And our job, Sammy, is to cut down through the sapwood and get at the hard heart of the tree if we want to kill it, or even to do it good. We have to find out the name of the man behind the crowd of them. Who is that man, Tucker?"

"There's no man like that," answered Tucker.

"You and Pooch and Thurber," said Geraldi, "down here in the desert, and those other roughs up yonder in the mountains . . . you all just happen to be working together? You . . . to kill the son . . . and the rest of 'em to kill the father? Is that it? You want me to believe this?"

He made a swift stride toward Tucker.

"I'm sick with wanting to run this knife

into your murdering heart and then twist the blade of it!" said Geraldi.

Tucker jumped back until his shoulders smote the wall.

"Pull him off! Don't let him kill me! I'll talk!" he begged Wilkes.

Wilkes actually was on the point of intervening, his horrified glance fixed on the knife that Geraldi held. But he saw Geraldi wink, and that threw him back on his heels.

"Talk is what I want," Geraldi affirmed. "I suppose that I'm a fool, but I'll give you your life for some honest answers, not the sort of lies that you were giving me a minute ago. Somebody is behind this game. I want to hear the truth!"

"Yes," Ray Tucker answered. "Somebody's brain is behind it. There's somebody so big behind it that old Wilkes is no better than dead, and so is Sammy here. So are you . . . whoever you are . . . because you've taken such a hand in the deal. For that matter, so am I dead, because I'm talking this way to you."

Geraldi looked straight across at Sammy Wilkes and saw that the news was hardening the big fellow, instead of shaking or softening him.

"We'll start at the finish," Geraldi said. "Who is Wisner?"

"He's the president of the El Gato bank."

"How much would he pay you?"

"There's ten thousand in the job . . . that would be five thousand for Alf and five for me."

"For killing young Sammy Wilkes, eh?"

"Yeah, for bumping him off," Tucker admitted sullenly.

"That fish-faced fellow, Pooch, he was in on the job, too, eh?"

"Yes," agreed the prisoner.

"Ten thousand dollars is quite a price, Sammy," Geraldi said. "You ought to be flattered."

"I'm nearer dead than flattered," said Wilkes. "He came sneaking in here to brain me when I was boiled and asleep. He would have turned the trick, too, except that you were here. And you . . . I don't even know your name."

"We want the inside lining of Mister Tucker's brain," said Geraldi, "and the first thing is to find out about the mastermind behind all of this business. We have Mister Silas Wisner to go after, to round out the information. But we've got a lot more to pump from Tucker. You can start in, Ray. We want to know everything."

"You think it'll do you good," answered Tucker, "but all it'll do will be to put me in the same soup with the rest of you. He never can be beat. He never has been, and he never will be. He's got arms that reach clean around the world, and he's got brains that can kill you with thinking of you. You ain't any better than dead right now. Neither am I."

"That's all interesting," Geraldi said. "But we want facts."

"Lemme have a breath of air," said Tucker. "That's all I want. I wanna clear up my brain a little before I take a turn on the witness stand. I got plenty to say. It'll take some time in the saying."

He went to the window and stood there for a moment, breathing deeply.

"You've seen my dad?" Sammy Wilkes asked Geraldi.

"I've seen him, of course. He's going to be all right, if we can get back into the mountains before they manage to scalp him. All right, Tucker."

"Let him have a breather," muttered Wilkes.

"Don't waste your pity on snakes," said Geraldi. "What's he doing? Praying?"

For the big fellow at the window had slipped to his knees, and the upper part of his body now leaned out across the window-sill as though he were speaking to someone on the ground beneath.

Then Geraldi saw a thin red stain run trickling down the wall beneath the window. He got to Tucker with a bound, and rolled the loose weight of the man around until Wilkes, also, could see what had happened. The hilt of a knife protruded from above the heart of dead Ray Tucker!

# VII

## "MEETING AN EQUAL"

Ray Tucker seemed to be smiling placidly at the ceiling, his eyes half shut as though he were relishing certain information that was known to himself alone.

Geraldi, leaning from the window, looked anxiously up and down the side of the building, and along the street. He saw nothing move. Whoever had climbed up, cat-like, to the window must have heard some of the last words of Tucker, and waited to strike the fatal blow. Then, with silence and with powerful speed, he had vanished in the street, or through some window of that façade of the hotel.

"We've got to get out of here," Geraldi said. "There's a dead man here in your room. His body has to be found. Our yarn about how he was stabbed through the window will look pretty fishy. We've got to move."

"If I go," Sammy Wilkes said, "people will think I'm a murderer."

224

"They will." Geraldi nodded. "And if you stay, you'll be murdered. It's better to be alive and be considered a murderer than it is to be dead, eh? If your conscience is clean, public opinion can't hurt you."

Wilkes leaned above the face of the dead man.

"Don't seem possible," muttered Sammy Wilkes. "The bigness of him, one minute . . . and the next thing, he's like this. They'd get me the same way, and pinch me out like a smoking candle."

"Come along with me," said Geraldi.

"No. I won't come with you. I'm going to stay here and face the music. I won't turn myself into an outlaw. I don't care what the music plays, I'm staying to face it."

Geraldi stared hard at him. For his own part, Geraldi considered the law rather a reef to be wrecked on than a shore of salvation, and Sammy Wilkes's determination to stand the gaff amazed him. At last he said: "The yegg who's behind all of these crooks will be a pretty happy fellow when he learns that you've been put in jail on a murder charge. But if you're going to stay, it's finished. I can see that you mean what you say. I want you to tell me one thing first, if you can. Have you any idea why other people should want your father's cabin and farm up there on Saddle Mountain?"

"I got no idea in the world," said Sammy Wilkes.

"Did anybody ever offer to buy it?"

"Only one man, so far's I know."

"When was that?"

"Oh, about a year ago."

"What sort of a fellow was he?"

"He was just a greasy old prospector who wasn't chipping rocks any longer. He wanted to settle down, he said. And he liked the look-out from Father's farm. He had plenty of money, and he offered a mighty fat price, considering what sort of a lay-out it is."

"What did he offer?"

"Three thousand dollars."

"That's a good deal."

"But Father wouldn't take it."

"Why not?"

"Dad and my mother had lived some happy years there, together. Her grave is up the hill behind the house, and the whole place is sort of holy ground to Dad. Afterward, the prospector wrote us a letter and offered us five thousand."

"Five thousand?"

"Yes, though he said he knew that was a lot more than it was worth. But he said he wanted the right place to retire and settle down in."

"What sort of a looking fellow, and what was his name?"

"We only knew his first name. He called himself Gus and signed the letter that way. He was about forty-five. Kind of greasy and strong-looking. He had a forehead as big as your hand. Why do you want to know so much about him?"

"Because this fellow Gus is one of the gang, or the big chief behind it. He said he wanted to settle down, did he? But he was only forty-five and looked strong. Sammy, there must have been some other reason for him to want the cabin."

"What other reason could there be?"

"I don't know. I don't know," muttered Geraldi impatiently. "About Silas Wisner. Know where he lives?"

"Yes. In the biggest house in El Gato. On the corner, two blocks down the street, with a lot of trees growing around his place."

"I'm leaving, Sammy. For the last time, will you come along with me?"

A footfall came rapidly up the stairs.

"No," Sammy Wilkes reiterated. "I won't step out from here on the sneak and have folks think that I'm a murderer. I'll stay and take what's coming."

The footsteps came down the hallway now. They paused at the door, and a heavy rap sounded. More people were coming, running. Rattlings and softly thundering noises of feet rolled through the flimsy shack.

Geraldi ran to the window.

"Keep me out of it if you can, Sammy," he whispered, in passing Wilkes. "I'm not through. I'm with you to the last gun."

He leaped over the dead body of Ray Tucker, and slipped out the window as he heard a man shout from the hall: "Open this here door, Wilkes!"

The last he saw was the head and broad shoulders of Sammy Wilkes stepping forward to let in the forces of the law.

Geraldi, in his haste, almost lost his handhold. He swung by the fingertips of one hand from the window eaves, but regained his hold and ran like a monkey down to the street level.

Voices were brawling behind the lighted window above him. The whole hotel was waking up. Distinctly, he heard a man shouting from Wilkes's room a sentence that had the word "murder" in it.

Well, they had Sammy Wilkes and they probably would make it as hot for him as possible. And what had he, Geraldi, accomplished? He thought of that as he ran down the street.

He had left the mountains bent on saving Sammy Wilkes from the danger of a duel with a celebrated gunman. He had, in fact, prevented that fight, and later on he had kept a murderer's hand from Wilkes. But instead of a free man, he left Sammy now with prison immediately before him and perhaps hanging later on. He could not say that his work had been very successful, therefore. He gritted his teeth to think how far he still was from the trail of the major criminal.

Joe Thurber, Silas Wisner, Ray Tucker, Alf, Pooch, the prospector called Gus, they were all in the game that had to do with the possession of the little cabin and farm of old Wilkes. It was a proof that the deal was of a vast importance, but still Geraldi had to fumble in the dark.

The only step that he knew how to take was toward Silas Wisner, the banker. And now he found the dark trees of the Wisner place before him, and the height of the iron fence behind which were the grounds of the banker.

The iron fence was tall, it was ridged with sharp spikes above, and only a bird could have been happy in attempting the passage of it. Geraldi, after a glance at the glimmering iron and steel, did not expend the effort to scale it. Instead, he took from the loincloth that he was still wearing one of those slivers of steel, selecting the largest to probe inside the ponderous lock of the garden gate, and almost at once he was able to push back the panel, and enter. He took care to push the gate shut in such a way that the spring lock engaged again, then he went up the winding gravel driveway.

The desert came up to the very edge of El Gato and poured through its streets, very often, torrents of arid heat and sandy windstorms. But Mr. Silas Wisner had provided an oasis for his house. Constant irrigation accounted for the big trees that rose beside the driveway, and under them Geraldi stepped on the soft cushioning of a lawn, and breathed of the sweet, raw fragrance of newly clipped grass. Now the face of the house appeared, two stories high, with a verandah with wooden columns and windows on whose polished blackness the stars picked out tremulous highlights.

Geraldi climbed one of the verandah columns, came to a locked window, and with a few magic touches of one of his narrow blades of steel unfastened the catch.

The raising of the window cost him ten minutes of careful work, for it was strongly lodged, and he must lift it without making so much as a whisper of sound. When it was wide, he put in his head and shoulders. The air was hot and still; it had the odor that summer puts in a room that is not regularly aired. So he decided that the chamber must be unoccupied, and slipped through the window fearlessly.

He found the door, discovered that it was unlocked, and stepped out into a wide hall that ran the length of the upper story of the house and was dimly lighted by a single lamp which hung from the ceiling at the head of the stairs. The floor was carpeted. A gleaming balustrade of mahogany ran around the well of the stairs. The brass knobs of the bedroom doors were shining.

Mr. Silas Wisner was probably in one of those rooms. Which might it be? Geraldi knew that one of the front rooms was closed. He had just entered through it. So he went to the end of the hall to look out on the rear of the building. He saw there what he had half expected to find, a roof terrace built out over some of the first-story rooms. The terrace was looked upon by double French windows, and Geraldi felt reasonably sure that the master of the house would be found inside them.

The window from which he looked aside at the terrace was easily and soundlessly opened. He passed through it, swung himself hand over hand along a bit of trimming that made a ledge along the rear of the house, and presently had swung himself over the balustrade of the terrace.

It had been hard work for him. He dropped to his knees, breathing hard, but controlling that breathing somewhat for fear lest even that sound might carry into the bedroom of the banker.

Then, without a snarl, with only the noise of strong nails scratching the floor and the thudding of padded feet, a huge beast rushed at Geraldi out of the darkness. The eyes of the monster dog shone as with their own light. The gape of his mouth Geraldi could make out, also.

His first gesture went toward his revolver. But to make such a noise would be to rouse the house and therefore to abandon all that he hoped to gain here.

So he waited until the last moment of the charge, then swerved to the side and to his feet. The teeth of the dog closed only on the ragged sleeve of his shirt as Geraldi rose, his grip on the mastiff's throat. The big jaws were frozen together on the cloth as contentedly as though it were the flesh nearest an enemy's heart. And Geraldi was free to heave the lumbering hulk over the terrace rail.

The mastiff took the shirt sleeve with him, and still kept his grip on it so fast that he uttered no howl even while falling through the air. He struck on his side, with a hollow sound, like the beating of a huge drum whose head is loosely strung. The big dog got up again, after a moment, and went off, staggering. This battle had been too mysteriously short; the mastiff cast not even a single glance up toward the terrace from which it had been flung.

So Geraldi turned to the bedroom entrance again. To keep out mosquitoes, there was a thin-gauze curtain fastened over the French windows. He undid one of these curtains and slipped through, when a voice that was perfectly collected and roused, said: "Yes, Toby! Yes, boy! What's the matter? Have you torn that curtain again, confound you? Come here, sir. Come here, Toby!"

Geraldi came in answer to the call, low-bending, shuffling his feet.

"The dundering blockhead of a fool of a dog," the man from the bed was muttering half aloud. "If he's torn that curtain, I'll have mosquitoes all the rest of the night. I'm going to teach him a lesson, if it's the last act of my life. I'm going to take the hide off him."

He turned with a few grunts and a muttering, as he spoke, and scratched a match, which he held out toward a lamp that was on the table beside his bed.

Geraldi, as soon as the light appeared, stood up from the floor, drew a revolver, and covered his man. He was seeing what might have stood as the face of one of the *conquistadores,* grown old. There was the same savage leanness of feature, the same pointed mustaches, the same wedge of gray beard. He felt what he had rarely felt in all his crowded life — that he was in the presence of an equal.

# VIII

## "ANOTHER KIND OF STRENGTH"

The wavering match light was now taken up by the sudden strong, broad glow from the lamp. The ceiling was whitened, the carpet glowed underfoot, the posts of the big mahogany bed were burnished, but most of all the eyes of the old man glittered as he sat up with a dog whip in his hand. He looked not at the gun but at the face of Geraldi.

"Got a revolver under that pillow?" asked Geraldi.

"No," said the other.

"Don't lie to me, Mister Wisner. However, it doesn't matter very much. Just keep both your hands in sight . . . that's the safest way."

As he spoke, Geraldi caused his weapon to disappear inside the loose folds of his shirt. As it vanished, there was a sudden twitching of the fingers of the old man, but he controlled the impulse that had almost mastered him. He regarded the naked left arm of Geraldi, slender, covered with sinuous ripplings of muscle.

"You know me, do you?" he asked.

"Yes," Geraldi answered.

"How did you get in? Through the door? No, I see the curtain's unbuttoned at the window. You came in from the terrace, eh?"

"Yes."

"Chloroform the dog, out there?"

"Did you ever try to chloroform a big, active mastiff with four feet and a jaw as strong as an alligator's? No, I threw him off the terrace, and the ground spanked the wind and the fight out of him."

"You threw him off, eh? No trouble for you to handle a hundred and seventy pounds of fighting mastiff, eh? Who the devil are you, eh? But that doesn't matter. You've come to rob me, I suppose? You'll get damned little for your pains."

"I haven't come to rob you, Wisner," Geraldi corrected. "I've come to be paid off."

"You never worked for me."

"I've worked for your boss."

"Boss? I have no boss!"

"No?" Geraldi spoke, and he permitted himself to smile with much hidden meaning.

He took from his pocket a small bit of paper and tossed it onto the bed. Wisner read it, and shook his head.

"I don't know anything about this," he declared.

"You know ten thousand dollars' worth about it," answered Geraldi. "I've come for the cash, and I'm going to have it." He did not raise his voice, which made his surety seem the greater. "Besides," he added, "if you don't pay . . . you'll get hell. You know that."

"You're just talking and talking, young man," said Wisner. "I don't know what you've done that would interest me."

"I've killed Sam Wilkes," Geraldi responded.

"Killed . . . ," began Silas Wisner. "What is that to me?"

"You want some proof?" asked Geraldi. He frowned, and, putting his luck on a far chance, he said: "How pleased would Gus be about this?"

Wisner sat suddenly very straight.

"You mean who? Gustavus. . . ."

"Yes," said Geraldi.

"Gustavus Rann, eh? He sent you! Well . . . well . . . well!"

He scratched in his beard and stared at the rags of Geraldi.

"I've done the job," Geraldi said, exultation rushing out into his voice. For, in fact, he had already gained what he had come for. He had found the name of the power behind all this plotting against the Wilkes family. Gustavus Rann! Somewhere he had heard that name. It was vaguely in his mind, a great, dim thing like a thunderhead on a far horizon. Gustavus Rann — that was the greasy prospector who had offered to buy the Wilkes' place — that was the master of Joe Thurber, Ray Tucker, and the rest, the master, too, as it seemed, of the wealthy banker, Silas Wisner.

"You've killed Sam Wilkes, eh?" asked Wisner.

"Yes. I've told you that."

"You've told me that . . . but the telling isn't the killing."

"No?"

"I want some proofs. You can wait till the morning when the news is sure."

"I wait till the morning when they'll have a rope around my neck!" Geraldi exclaimed. "No, I'm going to have my pay, and have it now. I'll show you the proofs. Here."

He took from his pocket the money that he had collected from Thurber. It made a comfortable wad. This he shook in his left hand, as he went on: "You know that Sam Wilkes made a big winning at roulette tonight. Well, here it is!"

"You might have picked his pockets without cutting his throat," objected Wisner. "The fool was getting two-thirds drunk, the last I heard of him. Besides, if you had killed him, you must have had help to do the trick. Just how did you get at him?"

"I climbed the side of the hotel and slid in through his window."

"Which window?"

"Second from the south corner, in front."

"Well, that's the window, well enough," agreed Wisner, who seemed impressed by this. "What did you do after you got into the place?"

"He was snoring in his bed. I fumbled until I had the outline of him. Then I pulled back the blanket. Wool is likely to spoil your stroke, with a knife. After that, I slid the blade through his heart."

Wisner licked his lips, and smiled a little.

"I think you could do a thing like that," he agreed. "Show me the knife, though. Or did you leave it sticking in the wound?"

"I'm not such a fool," Geraldi answered.

He pulled out the knife that had wounded Alf, and tossed it, hilt first, onto the bed beside Wisner. The latter picked it up, squinted at the blade, and then saw something that made him rub the side of the blade with the tip of his finger. He examined the tip with his finger, close to the light.

"Blood," he murmured. And he licked his lips again. "Well, here you are," Wisner said, offering the knife back.

"Throw it," said Geraldi.

A glint flickered across his eyes, and he flung the weapon with a sudden, unexpected turn of his wrist. Yet Geraldi did not flinch. He reached for that streak of light, and caught the knife by the handle, and then made it disappear as the revolver had done.

"Good!" said Wisner. "Good, and very good! You could be a useful young man . . . very useful. That trick is worth part of ten thousand. You may get your money, after all. Not ten thousand. Not all of that. But five thousand on the head. And if there's more coming later on, you'll certainly. . . ."

He began to get out of his bed. His scrawny, blue-veined foot appeared, fumbling at a slipper on the floor.

"Gus swore that there'd be no trouble about cashing in that note," Geraldi declared, "as soon as there was the right kind of blood on it. I'm going to have the full ten thousand, or else I'll raise such hell that you'll wish you were dead."

Wisner, fitting the second slipper on his

other foot as he sat on the side of his bed, squinted up into the face of Geraldi, and grinned suddenly, so that beard and mustaches bristled.

"A young wildcat," he said with admiration. "Young, lean, fast . . . and hungry!"

He stood up and reached for a linen dressing gown, and began to draw it over his arms.

"Where were the rest of 'em?" he asked.

"Tucker and Alf and Pooch . . . three soggy fatheads," Geraldi stated. "I don't know what Gus is thinking of, when he starts fellows like that on the job."

"He wanted the job done pretty fast. So he used numbers," Wisner said defensively. "Don't think that you can teach Gustavus his business, my lad. You're a bright fellow, but not a. . . . What's your name, by the way?"

"Jim."

"Jim what?"

"Slick Jim, some people have called me. I've had plenty of names. I've had more names than I've had suits of clothes. Now I'll take that ten grand."

"Come with me," said Wisner.

He led the way out of the room, and into the hall beyond, with Geraldi stepping soundlessly behind him. They passed down the stairs, Wisner in deep contemplation, occasionally shaking his head. On the first floor of the house, they came to a narrow door, which Wisner opened, and beckoned to his guest to enter.

"I follow the leader," Geraldi advised warily.

"That's all right," Wisner said, chuckling. "The door's narrow, and it's low, and I can tell you that a lot of great men have humbled themselves and bowed their heads and come in sidling, to enter that room. They came in with their hats in their hands . . . and they begged. I'm not a giant of strength in my hands. But there is another kind of strength . . . yes, there's plenty of another kind of strength."

He threw Geraldi a glance that was brilliant and poisonous with a malicious joy, and then led the way into the room.

# IX

## "THE TREASURE ROOM"

They entered a mere cubbyhole with a small table on which stood a pair of lanterns, one of which was lighted by the host. He then pulled on an iron ring in the floor, and a trap door opened — a door with a small steel grating set into the face of it, looking very much like the grill of a hot-air vent for heating the place.

There now appeared a steep flight of steps down which Silas Wisner passed. Geraldi descended behind him into a dim well of coolness. It was a cellar room with a high ceiling. The walls were cut into living rock, and only the ceiling was of wood. That wood, however, was ponderous, half a dozen great beams crossing from end to end to support the flooring above. In the nakedness of this chamber there were exactly three items of furniture — a small table and a chair, and a huge safe with a combination lock.

"It used to be a cistern," Silas Wisner explained complacently. He raised the lantern, and threw the light of it around the place. "If a thief tries to burrow into this, he'll need steel claws and a lot of 'em," said Wisner. "This well was cut into solid rock in the old days when time didn't matter. There's the first entrance . . . that trap door, up there, with the big padlocks on it."

"Suppose," Geraldi interrupted, "that a fast man with a gun put a bullet through you while you had the door of the safe opened?"

"Every sound bigger than a common speaking voice," said Wisner, "drifts up out of this cistern to four men who are sleeping right overhead. It would take them about half a second to block the entrance."

He grinned at Geraldi as he said this, and Geraldi grinned feebly back.

"I think I could work up a scheme to beat you at this, though," Geraldi said.

"You're welcome to try it, Jim," answered Wisner. "I've had a good many first-rate crooks try their hands at this cellar combination of mine. And they've all failed . . . they've all failed."

He was still speaking as his hands worked at the combination. Geraldi's eyes narrowed to thin slots of light as he concentrated to watch the numbers at which the pointer stopped. Even his eyes could not find them all, however.

The big door of the safe opened and showed inside, the bright steel faces of the inner chambers and drawers.

"With a can opener and about ten minutes of time," Geraldi commented, "I could help myself to a lot of interesting information there."

Wisner turned his head, and grinned over his shoulder. He seemed delighted by this conversation about the possibilities of breaking into his treasure.

"Oh, there's plenty to make it worth your time," he said. "You'd find some mortgages that wouldn't do you a great deal of good, and there are some other securities that you couldn't cash, but there are others, of course. Lots of others. You could turn them into coin in no time. And, besides, there's the quantity of the jewels, and the stacks of the hard cash. Hard cash, young man, in bales that would choke you."

"I believe you," said Geraldi. "I can read the mind of that safe by the good, honest, bright face of it. Someday, Wisner, I may come here alone and have something to say to it."

"I'm an old man, Jim," Wisner said, "but I have ways of giving you a reception that would touch your heart. I'll welcome the day when you try your clever hand here.

Other fellows have tried, also. And I gave them all the good time they were looking for. Plenty of excitement. Loads of it! So much excitement that they died of it, Jim."

He rubbed his bony hands together and began to laugh, letting his head roll a little from side to side on his scrawny neck. He looked to Geraldi like a medieval devil, one of those draped skeleton forms that wear a human head.

"All right," said Wisner. "Here is the money."

He unlocked a drawer, as he spoke, and opened it a little, made a brief selection among the contents, and then brought forth four narrow sheaves of banknotes with brown paper wrappers around them. He tossed them carelessly onto the table and slammed the drawer in and locked it.

Geraldi paid no heed to the packages of money. He knew that they would total ten thousand dollars, but there was a new wine running in his blood now, and a savage pricking of desire to lay his hands on the hoarded wealth that was accumulated here. If Wisner were the banker who supplied the needs of the great Gustavus Rann, vast must be the calls upon him, for even crime generally needs money to make money. It might not be limited to Rann alone. Perhaps there was here a central source, a great, high divide from which many rivers flowed, and all of them evil! And like a frigate bird from his lofty sky-blue tower, seeing far off a whole flock of fish hawks rising from the waters, dim forms guessed at through the mist, so Geraldi's mind was thronged with wild ideas of battle with many forces and glorious danger and a great reward.

What Wisner saw in the face of Geraldi was merely a slight quivering of the nostrils and a gleam of the eye, but the evil old man understood what temptation must be working in the mind of his guest, and smiled.

"You're not the first that I've brought down here. It works on the blood of the best of the boys. There was one took a shot at me, though he knew that the house above him was full of my men. He was so hungry to get at the safe that he missed me, however. I dashed out the lantern, and, while he started fumbling for me in the dark, my men came down with another lantern and caught him. He fell over there, in front of the safe. I remember that he lay kicking quite a while, and screaming . . . because he was shot several times through the body. Then there was another ambitious young man who remembered that a knife is more silent than a gun.

He threw his knife with a good aim, but it stuck in my arm that I raised to guard myself. And the yell I gave brought down my guards. He died painlessly, however, because the very first bullet split his skull. And perhaps you'll be a third, Jim?"

He began to rub his left arm gently, perhaps caressing the scar of the knife wound, and Geraldi wondered a little at him.

"No, Wisner," he said. "I'm not enough of a fool to charge my head against a stone wall. But later on you may hear from me."

He gathered up the packages of money and put them away.

"Wait a moment," said Wisner. "Young Sammy Wilkes took twenty-eight hundred dollars from the roulette game tonight. You say that you have the money. So I'll count it to see how it tallies."

Geraldi smiled upon him.

"I have my pay, Wisner," he said. "Why should I put part of it back in your smart hands?"

"Ten thousand dollars!" said Wisner. "It's a great deal of money for the killing of any fool!"

"But think of the stake that Rann is playing for," Geraldi said, once more fumbling in a darkness out of which he hoped to draw much information.

"What do you know about the stake that Rann is playing for?" Wisner asked sharply.

He slammed the door of the safe. It closed not with a metallic crash, but with a great soft puffing sound as it shut against a cushioning of imprisoned air. He spun the knob of the combination, still keeping his frowning face and the question in it turned toward Geraldi.

"What do I know about Rann's stake?" repeated Geraldi. "Why, Wisner, you don't think that a fellow like me would go into this sort of a game on a cash-and-carry basis? No, sir. A partnership is what I demand every time."

"Partnership? Partnership?" exclaimed Wisner. "Rann never takes in any partner except. . . . Well, what sort of a partnership did he offer you?"

"Ten percent," Geraldi replied instantly.

"Ten percent?" muttered Wisner. "It's not a great deal."

"Ten percent is plenty for me. If you know anything about the deal, you know that ten percent will be a fortune."

"What do you know about it?" asked Wisner. "You mean to tell me that Gustavus Rann would take in a new man like you and tell you everything?"

The idea seemed to irritate him greatly.

Again Geraldi guessed and fumbled in the dark. He said solemnly: "You know, Wisner, that there's more money in the scheme than your safe would hold."

Wisner's sharp eyes relaxed their grimness for a moment.

"Rann knows his own business," he growled. "But I'd call him a fool for telling any man as young as you about the stake he's playing for. It was another fool move to raid the house and burn it. A damned fool move! It's likely to bring people around the ruins. Likely to start them digging around among the embers, and, if they dig deeper than the charcoal and ashes, they'll be in that pay dirt. Not everyone is as blind as the Wilkes crew. Not all of 'em would live on top of a placer mine all their lives without suspecting it."

The light that struck in upon Geraldi's mind once more fairly blinded him. He began to laugh heartily, but almost soundlessly. The simplicity of the explanation amazed him. Yet what else but a mine could have made the little cabin and the mountain farm of old Wilkes desirable to Gustavus Rann? "A sort of a greasy-looking prospector," young Wilkes had called him. And a prospector he had been, indeed. The whole idea was now in Geraldi's hands, and he laughed to himself.

Wisner laughed, also.

"That's what I say. It's funny to think of an honest old fool like that living on top of a million dollars and never guessing it."

"A million? There ought to be more than that!" said Geraldi.

"Rann is always too much of an optimist," said the banker. "But I know something about this sort of business. Divide all the expectations by ten, and you're apt to come out closer to the final result."

Old Wisner was still chuckling over the folly of the Wilkes family, when Geraldi heard something at the head of the stairs like the noise that wind makes in the far distance, a faint whispering noise. If he had not been born with the ear of a wolf and the caution of a hunted deer, he would never have turned, as he did now. He saw dimly in the dark square at the top of the steps the flash of steel.

As one feels the direction of an eye, so Geraldi felt the direction in which that revolver was aimed, and leaped to the side. It spoke at the same instant, sending a bullet past his head, filling the room with the bellowing uproar of echoes that crowded against one another in their many repetitions. That uproar had hardly begun before

Geraldi's revolver was adding to it. Four bullets he fired as rapidly as his thumb could flick the hammer of the revolver. The last of those ounces of lead *clanged* against the steel under-facing of the cellar doors, as it was dropped into place.

# X

## "RANN'S TERMS"

Wisner stood back in front of the safe door, with his arms folded. Geraldi took a position near him. From this place they could not be easily covered through the grating in the cellar door.

"What's it all about?" Wisner asked with a wonderful calmness.

"There's quite a lot behind it, I'm afraid," said Geraldi. "But other people are likely to tell you about it."

"Whatever rascals tried to murder you, my men will take charge of 'em. They'll sweep 'em out of the way."

"Don't be too sure. There may be a man up there now your fellows would obey sooner than they'd obey you," suggested Geraldi.

"Who do you mean?" asked Wisner.

At this, a voice spoke through the grating. "Oh, Wisner!"

"Gus!" cried Wisner.

He started forward. But Geraldi caught

him firmly although gently by the shoulder.

"Stay here, Wisner," he commanded. "I need your company now."

Wisner looked blankly at him, at the same time explaining: "Hello, Gus! What set of fools tried to shoot down Jim? I'm down here with Jim."

"You are? Which Jim?"

"Your Jim. The fellow who's killed Sammy Wilkes for you."

"That's what he told you, eh? And you were fool enough to believe him?" came Rann's voice.

Sammy Wilkes had spoken about the greasy appearance of Gustavus Rann. And his voice had a greasy sound, also a husky, babbling quality, as though the man had just risen from the table.

"Was I a fool?" asked Wisner. He lowered his head a little, and looked up at his companion.

"You weren't a fool," Geraldi said. "You were just out of luck."

Wisner pulled out a handkerchief and began to rub it vigorously across his forehead.

"That fellow Jim who reported that he had killed Sammy Wilkes . . . do you want to know Jim's last name, Silas?"

"Yeah, I'd like to know."

"Geraldi is the name, Silas."

"Ah, ah, ah," Silas Wisner said, his voice ending in a groan. "And I. . . . Gus, he's in rags! And Geraldi's a dandy. I never could have guessed."

"Geraldi," Gustavus Rann said, "is always what other people don't expect him to be, and generally where they don't want him. Geraldi, I've never seen your face. It would be a pleasure to have a look at you."

"Thanks, Rann," said Geraldi. "I'd like to see you, too. But we'd better wait for the daylight."

"There'll be no daylight," answered Rann. "You're about to die, Geraldi, unless you can make certain terms with me."

"Wait a minute, Gus," broke in Wisner.

"Well?" asked Rann.

"If you try to kill Geraldi, how can you save me?"

"I can't save you, Silas," said the voice of Rann. "I'm sorry, but I can't save you."

"Oh, you damned blackguardly traitor!" yelled Wisner.

"Steady, steady," Rann said reprovingly. "You know we've always agreed that, if one of us made a fool of himself, the other had a right to shake him off like dust on the shoes."

"I've made no fool of myself!" cried

Wisner. "I've made no more of a fool of myself than you have. You let him find out your name . . . you told him about the pay dirt that the Wilkes house is built on . . . you allowed him ten thousand dollars for killing Wilkes . . . you gave him a note to me . . . you offered him a ten percent partnership with you, in the profits, and you made that offer without consulting me. Now you happen to discover, at the end of all this, that the man is really James Geraldi . . . and you dare to call me a fool."

"You old, white-headed jackass," Rann answered soothingly, "didn't you hear me say, a while ago, that I never laid my eyes on the face of Geraldi, or he on me? That's the truth. He came down here in the dark. He knew nothing. And he's probably pulled out all your information from your vest pocket. He's done such things before."

"He couldn't have done that," said Wisner. "He couldn't. . . ." He paused, agape. His eyes were blank as his mind went back over the strange events of that night. Suddenly he cursed, one deep-voiced syllable.

"Sorry," said Geraldi. "But it's true that I was all in the dark until you helped me out of it."

Wisner said nothing.

"Are you satisfied that you've played the fool, Silas?" demanded Rann.

Wisner maintained his silence.

"One of my friends, Joe Thurber, was stopped by Geraldi on his way into El Gato. But afterward, he slipped into the town. It was Thurber who climbed up to the room of Sam Wilkes and killed the traitor, Tucker, just when Ray was about to talk over everything with Geraldi. Thurber's here at my side now, and Sam Wilkes is in prison on a charge of murder. But old Wilkes himself, whom the fellows in the mountains left for dead, was saved by Geraldi, and now his cabin is provisioned, and he has a fellow to take care of him . . . a fellow a little bit sharper than a lynx. I want you to have the whole picture in mind. There probably is not enough evidence to convict Sammy Wilkes. Which will put us right back at the beginning of the job. All that we gain is wiping Geraldi out of the picture tonight."

He spoke gently, slowly, as though he were explaining a difficult problem to a child.

Wisner sat down in the chair and folded his arms. He demanded — and it was a statement rather than a question: "You wipe me out in wiping out Geraldi."

"If Geraldi will listen to reason,"

Gustavus Rann said, "you'll both be saved."

"Listen to reason? Aye, he'll listen to reason," said Wisner.

He turned grimly on Geraldi.

"What's your deal, Rann?" asked Geraldi.

"You've been a useful fellow to yourself and to the law," Rann replied. "Now I'll give you your freedom if you'll be useful to me."

"You want me to be a hired man?" asked Geraldi.

"Yes. But big pay. Commissions, not a salary. I have ideas, Geraldi. The two of us together could crack the world like a nut and get at the kernel."

Geraldi sat back against the wall and folded his arms. He looked at Wisner, then at his own thoughts.

"Hold on," muttered Wisner. "You're not hesitating, Geraldi?"

Geraldi shrugged his shoulders. Then he answered: "I'm sorry for you, Wisner."

The old man leaped to his feet in a frenzy. "Are you going to let yourself be murdered, instead of taking a chance to be rich?"

"I've had the sort of riches that I want," answered Geraldi. "Your thugs and yeggs, your murderers and gunmen, they've run like rats and mice when they saw me coming. That made me richer than money could make me, Wisner. If I join Rann. . . ."

"Be quiet," Wisner murmured. He drew close. He clawed at the arm of Geraldi and whispered in his ear: "Once you're out of this place, you can do as you please. You can promise anything. Swear whatever he wants you to answer. That won't hold you, once you're free. Any oath taken under compulsion . . . why, the law itself makes a man free from such a promise."

He panted in the eagerness of his speech. Then he drew back and saw on the face of Geraldi a peculiar calmness and cold resolution.

"What's your answer?" pleaded Wisner.

"It's this way," Geraldi said gently, almost apologetically. "I've gone free all my life. I've done as I pleased. I've been a picklock, and a second-story man. I've had my gunfights and my knife fights. I've been confidence man and a sharper. Honest men never suffered because of me. It's true that only the crooks have had any reason to curse me. But I've been a wild horse and never worn harness. There's only one clean thing for me to be proud of. I've kept my word. I've never broken a promise. If I take an oath to Gus Rann now, I'll be tied to him, and I won't be able to break the tie. And I'd rather be dead than herd with the crooks

I've been hunting down all my life. I'm sorry, Wisner. It may sound like crazy talk to you. But that's the point where I have to stick."

He expected a frightful clamor of expostulation from Wisner, but the old fellow uttered not a word. He merely turned a yellow-green and bowed his head to the inevitable.

"Well," called the voice of Gustavus Rann, "what have you two old cronies decided?"

"I can't take your job, Rann," Geraldi responded.

"Ah?" answered Rann. "I half expected that you wouldn't. Matter of principle, eh?"

"Call it what you want."

"Any matter of principle that refuses to let you turn old Wisner loose?" asked Rann.

"I'm sorry about Wisner," said Geraldi. "I suppose the old spider has sucked the blood out of a good many people, in his time . . . but just now I'll have to use him if I try to escape."

"Try to escape?" cried Rann. "Are you fool enough to think that you can escape, Geraldi? Don't you see that not even you can get out through solid rock? And the ceiling is about eighteen feet above the floor."

"Well," Geraldi said, "I'll have to take my chance, even if it's only one in a million. And if I die, this old rat dies with me."

He saw Wisner nodding, as though the banker understood the fatal justice that lay behind this attitude.

"All right, fellows," Rann said, his voice as casual as ever. "We might as well start. Have you opened up the faucet that leads to the roof cistern? Then turn the thing loose. It'll soon be over."

"What's the idea in his head?" Geraldi asked of Wisner.

The old banker remained seated, slowly shaking his head from side to side.

"You'll see," he said.

The next moment, water burst from a point high up on the wall and fell with a roar upon the stone bottom of the chamber. The spray whipped Geraldi's face. So fast was the influx that almost in a moment he was wet to the ankles. The stone felt slippery as grease under his feet.

"You've got some bullets left," Wisner said, speaking loudly but calmly above the noise of the falling water. "That's a better way than drowning like a pair of rats."

But Geraldi hardly heard him. He was staring up at the second trap door and at the four great, rusted padlocks that secured it.

Suddenly he took Wisner by the shoulder and shook him.

"Aye?" said the old man.

"Look up there at the second trap. The locked one."

"What of it?"

"Has it any more locks . . . on the outside?"

"Why put locks on the outside? So they could be tinkered with?"

"Where does that door open?"

"Into the storeroom."

"Then that's our chance, Wisner."

"If you had a hammer and chisel to break the locks open, maybe . . . and if you were a bird to fly up through the hole."

"I didn't say it was a good chance. It's the one chance in a million. Come here and get to work."

"I haven't the key to the locks," said Wisner. "Even if you could get up to 'em."

"Don't ask questions. Do what I tell you."

With that, Geraldi dragged the table to a point exactly under the padlocked trap door. The water was already halfway up the calf of his leg. On top of the table he placed the chair.

"Get up and stand on the chair," he ordered Wisner.

The old fellow looked narrowly at him.

Then, silently, he clambered up to the required position. Geraldi shook his head as he eyed the gap that still remained between the shoulders of Wisner and the ceiling. There was one reassuring token to him, and that was the surprising strength and agility that the banker had shown in mounting to his present place.

Onto the table, Geraldi sprang, with the hoop of the lantern over his left shoulder. He stepped onto the chair, huddling close to Wisner.

"I'm going to try to get up on your shoulders," he said. "I'll balance myself as well as I can. Put your feet on the edges of the chair. Brace yourself as well as you can . . . and if you fall, we're done for."

Then, resting the weight of his hands on Wisner's shoulders, he raised himself with one foot on the top of the chair's back. He lifted the other naked foot, and almost like a monkey's foot it gripped Wisner's hip. Slowly, fighting for perfect balance with every new move, Geraldi climbed until his knees were on the shoulders of Wisner. He reached up, and found that his hands were still far from the padlocks on the trap. So he rose gradually until his feet were planted on the shoulders of Wisner.

He felt great shuddering waves pass

through the banker, as the weight told on his old legs.

"Steady," Geraldi advised. "Steady, and hold hard."

He reached up, and found that he could easily grasp the nearest padlock. The instant he accomplished that, his balance was secured. There was a groan of relief from Wisner.

Geraldi's fingers were already working with one of those fragile pieces of steel, and, as it moved inside the keyhole of the lock, he gritted his teeth — for everything was clogged with rust.

He had to put away the picklock, unscrew the cap of the lantern's oil well, and pour into the palm of his hand four successive portions of the kerosene. This he decanted in turn, with all possible care, into the locks. Properly, he would have liked to soak the locks for hours, but he had only minutes instead. With the cap screwed back into place on the lantern, he resumed the work of reading the mind of the first padlock.

"Are these locks the same?" he asked Wisner.

"No. They're all different. You'll never make 'em out," said Wisner. "But go on trying. The water . . . it's almost up to the top of the table."

The kerosene, or the desperation that was in the fingers of Geraldi, suddenly freed the first lock, and he read the mind of the maker with wonderful admiration. It yielded, and he pulled it open and tossed it aside. It fell with a plump into the rising water.

"Go as fast as you can," urged Wisner. "The water's coming up . . . and my knees are beginning to give."

"Starch your knees stiff . . . and bear up!" commanded Geraldi. "We can't afford to be weak."

He opened the second lock with such speed that his heart leaped with a great hope. It fell. He heard a muttered thanksgiving from old Wisner. But now there was a continual shuddering vibration of weakness in the banker, as he supported the burden of Geraldi's weight.

The third lock was larger than the first two. It was more rusted also, and built upon an entirely different principle. Eagerly Geraldi dug into it. Twice he thought that he felt something give, and twice it proved to be no more than the dissolving of the rust inside.

The falling of the water no longer made a loud noise, for that which fell was received almost immediately by the surface of the inundation in the room. Geraldi could hear old Wisner panting with his effort. And still the third lock refused to be solved.

"I'm going fast . . . I can't stand!" groaned Wisner, "and the water's up to my knees. It's climbing higher."

Geraldi looked down, and the lantern light flashed back to him like many evil eyes of creatures swimming in the pool.

That moment the third box gave way to him, and he tossed it away with a muffled exclamation.

"There's only one left. Bear up, Wisner," he said through his teeth.

"I'll bear up. God knows what sort of brains are in your fingers to do what you're doing up there. But go fast, Geraldi. The water's at my waist . . . it's at my chest. I'll be choking in another minute."

Geraldi had no need of urging. Then he heard a muffled cry beneath him, and the supporting shoulders of Wisner gave way. Down plunged Geraldi into the cold of the water, but came up again swimming strongly. He was in total darkness. There was a faint smell of oil from the extinguished lantern.

"Wisner!" he called.

He heard the old man answering faintly.

"I can swim," said Wisner. "And here's the table."

Geraldi found it at once, and the hard claw of Wisner clutching the edge of it.

"Now for your gun, Geraldi," said the banker, "before the water spoils the cartridges. Quick, man. You can find my head in the dark. Put the muzzle against my temple, and pull the trigger. It's better to go that way than by choking in the dark."

"We've still got a chance," Geraldi tried to assure him. "A ghost of a chance. You can continue to swim?"

"Yes. But what good is swimming? This place will fill up to the last inch. I know it. And that devil Rann knows it, too."

"Let me do the thinking for both of us," said Geraldi. "Steady, now. You start swimming in the direction of my voice, and we'll pull the table over against the wall, under the trap door. Then I can work on the fourth lock. The darkness won't bother me."

An exclamation in a strange voice came from the lips of Wisner. He began to strike out heartily, and Geraldi presently felt the smooth, cold stone of the well. He went on till he came to the corner, and, stretching up his hand, he found the padlocked trap door exactly as he had expected. He found the fourth lock, and, lying on his back on the table, he fell to work with the sliver of steel once more.

There was no sound of rushing water now, but only faint murmuring noises as the flood mounted higher and higher along the wall.

There were only inches remaining between Geraldi's face and the ceiling. Before they filled, he must solve the lock or drown. He heard old Wisner whispering a prayer. It was the strangest prayer that ever was uttered.

"God Almighty, there's no profit in killing such an old rat. Give me a second chance. I've still got teeth, and I'll try to use 'em in the right way."

Water had closed over the lips of Wisner, to judge by the spluttering sound he made next. His hand clutched at the shoulders of Geraldi, who could feel the clumsy tide rising to his chin.

And then the lock gave. Wisner was gasping close beside him, as Geraldi exclaimed: "It's the last lock! Now, if we can lift the door. . . ."

He put both his hands above his head and thrust with all his might. He felt the door yield and lift, but the force of his thrust drove him far back into the water.

He rose again, swimming strongly. His head struck the ceiling hard, but he was only half stunned. The desperate will to live cleared his brain, and his fumbling hands found the trap door again. This time he managed to get a finger hold on the lower ledge, and, thrusting up with his other shoulder, he found the door lifting. He put one hand into the gap and heaved hard. The door swayed up, and he was through the gap at once, like a slithering wet snake.

The room was not pitch dark. Through a crack one broad ray of light struck across the black gap of the trap door and gleamed on the oily swirling of the water.

There was no sign of old Wisner. Geraldi would have groaned, but he locked the sound back in his throat. All noises that he made might be dangerous now and draw down Rann's men.

Then he saw two withered, shadowy claws reach out of the floor. He grasped them, and drew Wisner swiftly out to freedom. On the floor the old man lay gasping, while Geraldi lowered the trap door and stood over it. Faintly, beneath him, he could hear the water licking at the ceiling of the old cistern.

He saw Wisner sitting up, propped on unsteady arms.

"Now, Wisner," he said, "what do you want to do? They think that the pair of us are dead. Suppose that you come with me to the sheriff's office . . . suppose that we come back here with enough men to throw a girdle around the house and close in on Gustavus Rann, and the rest of 'em?"

He waited vainly for an answer.

At last Wisner muttered: "Rann's got nothing against me, Geraldi. I made a fool of myself. Or rather, you made a fool of me. There was no other way for Rann to get you, except by drowning both of us. I don't blame him."

Geraldi whispered an exclamation of wonder. "Are you going back to him, Wisner?"

"Geraldi," said Wisner, "habit's stronger than life, at my years. And Rann's a strong habit with me."

# XI

## "GERALDI'S RUSE"

Geraldi plucked off his wet clothes, wrung them to a dry twist, and pulled them on again. He rolled up his trousers to the knees. Against the wall near the door, he found a slicker hanging, and he slipped this on over his clinging garments.

"I'll make a bargain with you, Wisner," he said. "You lie flat here for five minutes. Or else I try to take you out of this place with me, and arrange to have a public hanging for you."

"I lie flat," said Wisner. Then he added, with a burst of admiration: "There's my hand, Geraldi. You're walking off with ten thousand great big round dollars belonging to me, but I don't grudge 'em. You got me into this fix . . . but you got me out again. There's my hand."

"I'd rather shake hands with a bunch of rattlesnakes," responded Geraldi. "You'll be sinking your poison into the heart of some honest fellow before long. You'll be

271

sucking blood again, I know. And perhaps one of these days I'll have a chance to come back and get at you again. I'll tell you what . . . a man that does murder with a gun is a bright and honorable character, compared to the moneybags that hire the killing."

He left the hand of Wisner extended aimlessly in the air and moved to the door. Quiet sounds moved far away through the house, but nothing was nearby. So he opened the door soundlessly and stepped out into the hallway.

Straight opposite him a man demanded: "Who's there?"

Geraldi was in a broad hallway on the first floor of the house, dimly lighted from the lamp that burned at the first landing of the stairs. Facing him was a man with a sawed-off shotgun, which was held at the ready, pointing toward Geraldi. There was nothing in the world that Geraldi respected quite so much as a sawed-off shotgun.

"Where's Joe? Where's Thurber?" he demanded impatiently.

"I dunno. Who are you?"

"Go ask Gus Rann," Geraldi said with a pretense of heat. "Fetch Joe Thurber. Rann has an outside job for him and me. Get Thurber on the run. I have to wait outside."

"I guess I know what the job is," said the other, and straightway hurried down the hall.

Geraldi went to the front door of the house, pulled it open, and stepped out onto the verandah. The wooden pillars were pale stripes against the outer blackness. The trees rolled like small hills against the brightness of the stars.

Right beside the doorway, Geraldi waited. He could still feel clammy death, as it were, rising to his ears and his chin. He could still hear the lapping of the water against the walls.

It might be that the alarm was being spread inside the house at this moment, by old Wisner. It might be that the guard's report would excite suspicion, instead of bringing Joe Thurber. But still Geraldi waited, like one who has heard the bullets sing so often in battle that the sound is half despised and half welcome.

Then the door opened, and he saw the dull light from inside the house gleam on the face of Joe Thurber. As the man closed the door behind him, Geraldi nudged the muzzle of a Colt into his ribs.

"Take it quietly, Joe," he cautioned.

"Great guns," breathed Thurber, "it's his ghost!"

"Does a ghost handle a Forty-Five, Joe?" Geraldi asked, and jolted Thurber's ribs again with the Colt. "Shove up your hands."

Thurber raised them. He was so overcome that he wavered from side to side and seemed about to faint. Geraldi took one gun from his victim.

"Put your hands down," he commanded. "Walk straight before me down the drive. If you don't step soft . . . if you so much as cough . . . I'll leave you dead behind me."

Thurber obeyed. He walked with all the care of a stalking beast down the driveway, and they came to the front gate.

"Is this gate guarded?" asked Geraldi.

"No," Thurber muttered. "I don't think so." He added: "What're you going to do with me, Geraldi?"

"We'll see about that," said Geraldi.

The key was on the inside of the gate. It needed only to be turned, and they were on the outside, in the dust of the street.

"If I shot you through the heart and let you lie here," Geraldi said, "what would happen?"

"I know," said Thurber. "I can see the headlines. 'Famous gunman found dead.' They'd add up the list of gents they think

I've killed. They'd call it a good day for law and order."

"How many states want you for murder, Joe?"

"Only about three," said Thurber.

"Is this state one of 'em?"

"Yes."

"Will being held for one more murder matter very much to you?"

"No."

"You're going down to the jail with me," explained Geraldi. "You're going to give yourself up and confess who you are and how you killed Ray Tucker. Understand?"

"I put the rope around my own neck, eh?"

"After jail comes a trial," Geraldi continued. "Maybe your bright lawyers can get you free. Maybe the jail won't hold you. I don't care. What I want is Sammy Wilkes. Going to jail is better for you than dying here and now. And I'd like to do the killing of you, Joe. There's something in the tips of my fingers that would like to do it."

"I'll lead the way," said Thurber.

He walked straight down the street, turned through an alley, and came out on the little sandy plaza that was one day to be surrounded by the public buildings of the town of El Gato. The town had grown old, since that plaza was laid out, but nothing save the jail had ever been built. It stood in a big open space, surrounded by mesquite, instead of by a city hall and post office. It looked like any other house, except that the windows were so small and steel bars glimmered before them.

They walked up the steps, and Geraldi knocked at the door. He knocked three times before there was an answer. Someone called sleepily to know who was there.

"Somebody that needs to find the sheriff. Is he here?"

"No. He's home across the street."

"Which house?"

"The second one from the corner. With the tree in the front yard."

They found that house at once, and knocked at the door in turn.

Old Wisner, by this time, surely had given the alarm. And the great Gustavus Rann now doubtless understood who had asked for Joe Thurber on an "outside job." There would be no chance to surprise Rann and collect some of his gang. As for Wisner himself, what proof was there against him?

Geraldi was thinking of that when a voice answered his knock, and a quick step came down the hallway.

"Who's there?" called a strong voice, with no sign of sleepiness about it.

"There's Joe Thurber here, who wants to do some confessing," Geraldi replied.

The man inside the hall exclaimed something, and was instantly on the porch. He carried a rifle in his hand. He was a little man. Geraldi could make out a stoop in his shoulders, and the pale shadow of thin mustache across his face.

"Here's Thurber," Geraldi said. "Light a match and see for yourself. You're the sheriff?"

"Yes."

The match was lighted. One glimpse was enough for the sheriff, and then he turned the light toward Geraldi. The latter promptly blew out the flame.

"Who are you?" demanded the sheriff.

"I'm a friend," Geraldi said. "Anybody who brings you Thurber is a friend. Eh?"

"Maybe so. I'll take a look at you, though."

"Thurber will tell you about me, later on. Now, Joe, speak your first piece."

Thurber paused, and cleared his throat. Before he had finished, the sheriff had fitted a pair of handcuffs over his wrists.

It was then that Thurber said: "Well, you've got me. It's better than dying in the gutter like a dog. I'm Joe Thurber, all right."

"The first look at your pretty face, and I knew that," said the sheriff.

"There's more news for you," Thurber said. "I'm the fellow who shinnied up the front of the hotel and stabbed Ray Tucker."

"The devil you did!" said the sheriff. "What's this all about? What brought you here anyway?"

"Jimmy Geraldi . . . here beside me with a gun in his hand," groaned Thurber.

"Saying ain't just the same as doing," said the sheriff.

"I bought that knife from Pedro Oñate, right here in this town. Pedro will know. He's got his mark on the knife."

The sheriff groaned with astonishment.

"You'd rather take your chances with the law than with Geraldi? Is that it?" he asked. "Geraldi . . . are you really James Geraldi?"

"No matter about that."

"What do you get out of this, anyway?"

"I get Sammy Wilkes. I get him out of the jail right now."

"It ain't regular," complained the sheriff. "There's a regular form before I can. . . ."

"Suppose that anybody had offered you Thurber in exchange for Wilkes. Would you have taken him? And here's Thurber who confesses that he's done the job that Wilkes is jailed for. How does it sound to you?"

"It sounds good to me," the sheriff muttered. "I'm going to break the law to save the law. Come along with me. Geraldi, will you please step inside the house one minute, and have a drink, and let me take a look at you? I've surely been hearing enough about you."

"I'd rather stay in the dark down there on the street. I'll wait there for Sammy Wilkes," Geraldi said.

And there he waited, in the deep dust, working his naked toes in the liquid coolness of it, while the sheriff crossed the street.

Thurber spoke a brief farewell.

"You've beat me twice, Geraldi," he said. "And this time you've put a rope around my neck. But I'm not dead yet. Maybe I'll be able to do some little thing for you, before I'm finished. And if I can't, maybe my friends will turn the trick for me."

"I'm wanting to see your friends again, all of 'em," said Geraldi. "So long, Thurber."

He watched the door of the jail open and close on the new victim. He saw the door open again, and, after a moment, a tall man bounded down the steps.

# XII

## "GERALDI'S SHARE"

Not on a roan mustang, but on a tall black stallion that shimmered like watered silk, Geraldi rode again up to the edge of the clearing where stood the cabin of old Wilkes, beside the newly charred ruin of the barn.

The cow in the pasture chose this moment to bawl loudly. Its mooing wakened the echoes far up the steep hill slopes on each side, and the size of the sound seemed to make the brilliant sunshine tremble.

Geraldi, issuing on the black stallion from the trees, sat the saddle for a moment longer in that sunshine. He was dressed again in the clothes that he had cached near the death place of the roan. And he had again for a weapon the Colt revolver that was dear to his heart — the one with the sights carefully smoothed away. His own saddle was under him, and his own bridle reins were in his hands. Therefore, he felt complete.

There was only one trouble, and that was

the sense of weariness that, like a leaning wall, pressed against his brain and against his nerves, and made his muscles quiver.

Out of the trees behind him came big Sammy Wilkes, now looking thinner and older.

"Hold up there!" a voice shouted at them. "Lemme know who you are before you come any nearer to me!"

Geraldi saw that the door of the cabin was open, and that just within the shadows of the threshold stood the form of a tall man with a rifle in his hands. It was Hank, dutifully mounting guard.

"It's Hank!" called Sammy Wilkes. "Hey, Hank, don't you know me?"

He galloped his horse forward, and Hank came out into the sun, laughing with pleasure.

Sammy had bolted inside the house, while Geraldi shook hands with the guard he had hired.

"Seen anything around here since I last was with you, Hank?" he asked.

"Kind of some shadows, snooping the other day just after I got up here," replied Hank. "I sung out, and I didn't hear no answer. I put a couple o' rifle bullets where I thought I'd seen things moving through the trees. That was all. Maybe they was coyotes.

I dunno. But I went out this morning and scouted around, and I seen the sign where a couple o' men had been hanging around close."

"You've been on the job." Geraldi smiled. "Maybe you've saved your own scalp. Maybe you've saved old Wilkes's scalp, too. But I think that the danger's entirely over now."

"What danger was it? What was up?" asked Hank.

In his eagerness, he canted his head to one side, like an inquisitive bird of some gawky sort.

"We'll get the old man out here, and have a look," answered Geraldi.

He went into the cabin, to find that old Wilkes was sitting up in his bunk well propped for comfort, and smoking a pipe. There was already a color in his face, and a new light in his eyes.

Sammy, on one knee beside the old man, was saying eagerly: "His name is Geraldi. It was Geraldi that kept me from being murdered in the hotel. It was Geraldi that put Thurber into the jail in my place. He did everything! It's the real Geraldi!"

"It can't be," Wilkes was answering. "I don't care what he done, the real Geraldi is a pile bigger. There's more to him. The real

Geraldi is as strong as a hoss, everybody says. And. . . ."

He saw Geraldi standing in the doorway.

"Son," he said gently, "are you the real Jimmy Geraldi, that folks talk about so much?"

"I have much better news than names for you," answered Geraldi. "Sammy, give me a hand with him."

Between the two of them, they carried Wilkes out of the house and placed him in a chair out in front of it.

"He's going to do something. What is it, Sammy?" old Wilkes asked.

"I dunno," said Sammy. "He's promised to tell me what it was that those devils was after when they come here raiding you, and hitching Joe Thurber and his guns to my trail. Is that what you're going to show us now?"

"I'll try to," Geraldi said. He himself felt wonderfully tense. It was not mere weariness that put the pulse throbbing in his throat. He added: "We'll try to get the answer out of the ground. Sammy, get me a big washbasin, the biggest that you have, and a shovel, will you?"

The two were brought. And right before the threshold of the Wilkes cabin, Geraldi used the spade to dig up a foot or so of the close-growing turf. Under that upper layer of leaf mold appeared a fine dark sand with which Geraldi filled the basin.

"Come along with me," he said to Hank and Sammy. "I think there's going to be a surprise left at the bottom of this pan, and we'll bring it back to show your father."

So he led the way to the runlet of water, and at the verge of the pool he allowed the current to fill the basin and keep on running in. Dark clouds of the pulverized soil rose into the clear water like smoke into mountain air. The contents of the basin dissolved to half, to a double handful, to a slight sediment at the bottom of the pan.

It was Hank who shouted suddenly and loudly, so that everyone started.

"Gold!" he yelled.

And that word which had led millions around the world rang and echoed up the slopes.

Geraldi could see, then. The remaining sand was sprinkled with glittering yellow specks. As the last bit of it was carried off in the stream, there remained a thin yellow layer, wonderfully bright, that sparkled in the sunshine through the water.

Geraldi emptied out the liquid. He took the basin back and scraped into the horny palm of old Wilkes what made a tiny pyramid of glistening metal.

The hand of the old man was shuddering with joy. He closed his eyes, and the voice of Geraldi explained slowly: "That's the end of the business. That greasy fellow, that prospector who was up here and called himself Gus, was Gustavus Rann, the greatest crook in this part of the world. He found gold in the soil when he was here. I suppose something made him guess that the old worked-out diggings down the side of Saddle Creek were very like this place here. He did a little exploring and found out. Then, of course, his game was to get hold of your place, Wilkes. He wanted to buy it. When he found that you wouldn't sell, his next game was to get you and Sammy out of the way. He used Thurber to pull off Sammy. He sent some other devils to murder you while Sammy was gone. But he missed both times. You have a gold mine to pay you for a bullet through the leg. And there's nothing more that the great Gustavus Rann can do about the job, because now the world will know that the gold is here. He's played out his hand, and you've won the jackpot."

"We've won it!" exclaimed Sammy Wilkes. "Aye, and you've won, Geraldi! You've won an equal share . . . and even

285

that's a small way to try to pay you back."

"I've won my own little pile on the side," said Geraldi. "All that I want from you people is a chance for a long sleep."

He disappeared into the cabin as he spoke. Sammy, filled with wildest joy, would have followed to argue the last point, but his father stopped him.

"Folks like you and me, common folks," said old Wilkes, "we don't understand gents like Geraldi. We don't understand the way that they carry on. It ain't for gold that he goes hunting around the world. You and me, we've come to the end of the trail here, and we've got enough to make us happy. But this here trail for Geraldi . . . maybe it's just beginning. Who knows? Leave him be for a little while, Sammy. His mind is as much his own as his revolver."

# About the Author

**Max Brand**® is the best-known pen name of Frederick Faust, creator of Dr. Kildare, Destry, and many other fictional characters popular with readers and viewers worldwide. Faust wrote for a variety of audiences in many genres. His enormous output, totaling approximately thirty million words or the equivalent of 530 ordinary books, covered nearly every field: crime, fantasy, historical romance, espionage, Westerns, science fiction, adventure, animal stories, love, war, and fashionable society, big business and big medicine. Eighty motion pictures have been based on his work along with many radio and television programs. For good measure he also published four volumes of poetry. Perhaps no other author has reached more people in more different ways.

Born in Seattle in 1892, orphaned early, Faust grew up in the rural San Joaquin Valley of California. At Berkeley he became a student rebel and one-man literary movement, contributing prodigiously to all campus publications. Denied a degree because of unconventional conduct, he embarked on a series of adventures culminating in New York City where, after a period of near starvation, he received simultaneous recognition as a serious poet and successful author of fiction. Later, he traveled widely, making his home in New York, then in Florence, and finally in Los Angeles.

Once the United States entered the Second World War, Faust abandoned his lucrative writing career and his work as a screenwriter to serve as a war correspondent with the infantry in Italy, despite his fifty-one years and a bad heart. He was killed during a night attack on a hilltop village held by the German army. New books based on magazine serials or unpublished manuscripts or restored versions continue to appear so that, alive or dead, he has averaged a new book every four months for seventy-five years. Beyond this, some work by him is newly reprinted every week of every year in one or another format somewhere in the world. A great deal more about this author and his work can be found in *The Max Brand Companion* (Greenwood Press, 1997) edited by Jon Tuska and Vicki Piekarski.

We hope you have enjoyed this Large Print book. Other Thorndike, Wheeler or Chivers Press Large Print books are available at your library or directly from the publishers.

For more information about current and up-coming titles, please call or write, without obligation, to:

Publisher
Thorndike Press
295 Kennedy Memorial Drive
Waterville, ME  04901
Tel. (800) 223-1244

Or visit our Web site at:
www.gale.com/thorndike
www.gale.com/wheeler

OR

Chivers Large Print
published by BBC Audiobooks Ltd
St James House, The Square
Lower Bristol Road
Bath BA2 3SB
England
Tel.  +44(0) 800 136919
email: bbcaudiobooks@bbc.co.uk
www.bbcaudiobooks.co.uk

All our Large Print titles are designed for easy reading, and all our books are made to last.